THE PLAY

Brit Boys Sports Romance

J.H. CROIX

J.H. CROIX

To friends who make life better in all ways.

Sign up for my newsletter for information on new releases!

http://jhcroixauthor.com/subscribe/

Follow me!
jhcroix@jhcroix.com
https://amazon.com/author/jhcroix
https://www.bookbub.com/authors/j-h-croix
https://www.facebook.com/jhcroix
https://www.instagram.com/jhcroix/

Chapter One

LIAM

"Bloody hell," I mumbled. I gave my knee a test bend, only to grit my teeth at the bolt of pain.

"Easy mate," Alex said. "No need to be stupid about it."

I glanced to Alex and rolled my eyes. Alex Gordon was waiting with me at the sleek, state of the art medical facility in Seattle. I was sitting there with a badly twisted knee waiting for the surgeon who was supposed to work wonders and make me good as new.

"At least we won," I said, latching onto something other than the throbbing pain in my knee.

Alex chuckled and leaned his head against the wall behind him. Not for the first time, I was damn grateful he happened to be here with me. A month ago, we were signed to an American team on the heels of a crushing loss in a championship game in England. I'd known Alex since we were best mates in grammar school in a small town outside of London. We grew up playing football together, went to university together and got lucky enough to be signed to the same team back in England. Two months ago when my mum died from a stroke out of nowhere, I lost my focus, and our team lost its shot at the championship game. Before I came out of my stupor, our harebrained management ended our contracts and next thing I knew, my best shot at a good contract was with the Seattle Stars, a team paying big money for talent. Seeing as they signed me along with Alex and two other teammates from England, I went for it.

"It'd be nice if they called football by its proper name here," I said, my favorite complaint ever since we landed on American soil.

Alex ran a hand through his messy brown hair, giving a roll of his brown eyes. "Not happening, mate. American football is way more popular than soccer here."

"Bloody stupid to call it something else when everywhere else it's football," I mumbled.

He shrugged and moved on. "How's the knee?"

Alex knew as well as I did there was plenty to worry about with my knee. Many footballers had seen their career stall after a knee injury. A bad injury or a less than stellar recovery could mean reduced speed and reflexes, which could mean the difference between good and amazing. Elite players weren't good. They had to be amazing. The team's doctor had ridden with us on the way here, but he'd wandered off to find the surgeon who was supposed to work magic on my knee.

"Eh, hurts. Can't be too bad though. I walked off the pitch."

"Field, mate. It's a field here."

I elbowed Alex in his side, which was conveniently not the side with my bruised shoulder. A nasty collision with a defender sent me sideways, twisting my knee and jamming my shoulder into the ground. I was impatient and ready to see the doctor. Just as I started to wonder where the hell Dr. Monroe was, the door to the room where I'd been deposited with Alex opened.

I looked up into the most gorgeous pair of green eyes I'd ever seen. A woman walked through the door, and my mind was effectively blown with one look at her. Her eyes were bright behind her glasses. The wild, dark curls of her hair were partially tamed into a knot atop her head, yet a few curls escaped as if in defiance, one winding around the temple of her glasses. The curls dangled around her face, which was heart-shaped, her complexion pale with a few freckles scattered across her nose. Never one to shy away from a good long look, my eyes traveled down, taking in the woman's basic green hospital scrubs. It was hard to tell what her figure was underneath, although she was curvy enough her breasts were stretched against her top. All I could do was stare at her. For the first time since I'd collided with that defender on the pitch, I wasn't obsessing about what any of it might mean for my career.

Dr. Monroe stepped into the room behind the woman who'd paused by the door, her hands clasped together in front of her. Those green eyes of hers flicked from me to Alex, but her expression was hard to read. "Liam, this is Dr. Bowen. She's here to take a look at your knee." Dr. Monroe turned to the woman as he gestured to me. "This is Liam Reed."

I started to stand when it occurred to me that might not be the brightest idea. "Nice to meet you Dr. Bowen," I said with a wink.

I felt Alex's shoulders shake slightly with laughter beside me. Dr. Bowen adjusted her glasses, which were green to match her eyes and angled up at the corners slightly. "Nice to meet you Liam. Let's get you into the examining room here," she said, pointing to a door off the small waiting room.

Alex stood at the same moment Dr. Monroe stepped to my side. I wanted to brush them away, annoyed my knee was in enough pain I'd rather stay right where I was. I gritted my teeth and tolerated Alex's hand under one elbow while he walked beside me through the door into the examining room. The room wasn't large by any means. With two foot-ballers and a tall doctor in there with the lovely Dr. Bowen, there was hardly any room to move around the table in the center of the room.

I was accustomed to having people around me constantly when it came to the state of my health and playing. Dr. Bowen, on the other hand, didn't seem to think a group exam was a great idea. She adjusted her glasses again, tempting me to want to tug on one of her errant curls. "I'd like some privacy please," she said briskly.

Alex quietly turned and stepped out of the room. He was the tall, dark, quiet type, which was why he was such an amazing goalkeeper—calm and cool at all times. Dr. Monroe, on the other hand, turned his sharp eyes to Dr. Bowen. "Olivia, I'd like to be here for the exam," he said firmly, as if expecting no argument.

As a flush rose on her cheeks and her eyes narrowed, all I could think about was how perfect her name was for her. Olivia. Lust roared through me, followed promptly by a jolt of pain when I went to lean against the table.

Olivia basically had a stare down with Dr. Monroe. After several beats, she spoke again. "Whether you'd like to be here or not, it's not how I work. Liam is my patient, and I'd like to meet with him privately first. I understand you're the team doctor and would like to be involved in planning, but first I'd like to take a good look at his knee, review the MRI results and then we'll talk."

I bit back a grin because damn if her bossy side wasn't fun to see. I sobered immediately, realizing she was trying to do right by me and not just go along with whatever the team doctor, and by extension, management might want. After another brief staring contest, Dr. Monroe nodded and turned to leave. He glanced back at me before he closed the door. "Liam, if you need me, let me know."

I resisted the urge to roll my eyes. I knew Dr. Monroe meant well, but it's not like Olivia would hurt me. I was quite looking forward to a few private moments with her, although for all the wrong reasons. He closed the door behind him, and I turned to Olivia. I'd stopped even thinking of her in doctor terms and was busy wondering how the hell I could get her out of those scrubs.

She wasn't even looking at me and was clicking through some screens on a laptop on the counter. After a moment, she turned back. She held a pen in her hand and flipped it back and forth between her fingers. Her gaze coasted over me. I was sweaty and streaked with dirt and didn't give a damn.

"Well, Olivia," I said, emphasizing her name. "You wanted to meet with me privately. Here we are."

Her eyes widened and then narrowed. I could sense her wrestling with her thoughts, and it made me want to tease her even more. I felt let down when she simply shook her head slightly and stepped to my side. "Let's get you on the table." She moved efficiently and had me sitting on the table with my leg stretched out before I knew it. Her touch was cool and impersonal.

"I took a look at the MRI results from the scan they did before they brought you here. You tore your meniscus, but I'm guessing that doesn't surprise you," she said, her hand resting on my lower calf.

My gut clenched and an awful feeling of dread welled inside, sickening fear chasing fast on its heels. Football was my life. I didn't play for the fame, but I had it. It came with being one of the best midfielders in England and right up there in the world. A knee injury could spell the end of my career, and I was only thirty. I had plenty more years to play if I stayed healthy. I swallowed against the fear rising inside and met Dr. Bowen's gaze. She'd suddenly become Dr. Bowen in my mind again. I needed her to be that right now, so I could cling to the hope she could make me good as new. I'd been promised she was one of the best surgeons I'd find, and I prayed that to be true.

"Bloody hell."

Dr. Bowen's eyes softened, just the slightest bit. "I bet

that's how this news feels, but it doesn't have to. You're young and healthy as a horse. The tear isn't too bad. I'm confident we can have you back on the field within a few months," she said with a subtle nod.

"All I care about is playing again. If you can make that happen, I'll do whatever you say."

A smile played at the corners of her mouth. "Right then. Are you comfortable going ahead with the surgery? It will be an outpatient procedure. You'll need to plan for a day here and then we'll send you home. I have plenty more to review, but let's cover the big picture first."

I shrugged. "Of course I'm comfortable. Let's get this done. The sooner the better." I didn't voice aloud the jumble of worries crowding my mind. The underlying fear that I might be facing the end of my career was powerful and hard to ignore, but I couldn't let myself dwell on it.

"You know you can choose your own doctor," she said gently.

I stared at her, confused by her point. "Dr. Monroe says you're the best."

"He does, does he? Well, either way, it's up to you. It's your knee. To be honest, that's why I wanted to give you a few minutes to yourself. You sports guys are all but owned by the teams, so it's easy to forget when it's comes to your medical care, you call the shots."

Dr. Monroe's opinion aside, I didn't want anyone other than Dr. Bowen to operate on my knee. Something about how she stood up to Dr. Monroe cemented my trust in her. She was still Dr. Bowen at the moment. I nodded firmly. "It has to be you."

Those green eyes held mine and damn if the bloody woman didn't know how to keep her expression controlled. Whatever she was thinking was hidden behind a bland, somber gaze. She finally nodded. "Right then. Well, let's go over the particulars."

She rolled a wheeled stool to the edge of the counter and

perched on it. She adjusted those glasses again and spun on the stool with a computer tablet in hand. She briskly started talking, all business was definitely her mode, and reviewed the details of my surgery. I zoned out when she idly twirled one of those loose dark brown curls around her finger. After a few minutes, she set the tablet down.

"So will that work for your schedule?" she asked.

I'd noticed somewhere along the way, while she was driving me wild with her talk about the surgery, that her mouth was nearly perfect. When she was still, it was as if everything about her tightened up, so I hadn't noticed her lush, full lips at first. But when she started talking, she forgot to keep herself buttoned up. Her rosy red lips were distracting beyond belief. I'd swung my legs to the side of the table and was relieved, otherwise she'd have seen my how hard my cock was. Not that I was one to be shy when it came to women, but Olivia was a challenge and I knew it. She would most certainly not take well to blatant flirting. I stared into her green eyes and tried to recall what her question was.

"Come again?"

"The surgery. Will it work to do the surgery in two days?" she asked, speaking slowly, a flicker of annoyance in her eyes.

"Olivia," I loved saying her name and paused to enjoy it. At the arch of her brow, I grinned. "My schedule is your schedule."

Chapter Two

OLIVIA

I looked over at Liam Reed and had to fight to keep from returning his grin. He was devilishly handsome with his straight black hair, deep blue eyes, chiseled features and a body so muscled and fit, it was hard to keep from staring. I'd been working with athletes since my stint as a resident in medical school. I was quite accustomed to ridiculously handsome specimens who expected women to fall at their feet. Usually, their looks didn't draw my attention and their attitude often turned me off. Liam was another matter altogether. The moment he'd pinned his eyes on me, my body had tightened inside, heat unfurling from my center and radiating outward. It made me restless, prickly and annoyed.

So, I bit my lip and looked down at my computer tablet, clicking through a few screens. My actions weren't entirely pointless as I took another look at the MRI results. Medicine was my life and had absorbed most of my time, energy and intellectual capacity ever since I started college. I took comfort in the details of every case that I handled. My relentless attention to detail fit beautifully with orthopedic surgery. I hadn't set out to work with athletes, but that's where I'd landed. I'd graduated from medical school Summa Cum Laude and promptly walked into a position at Seattle Sports Orthopedics. At twenty-nine, I was the youngest doctor on staff there and constantly fighting to prove my worth. While I loved the surgery part of my job, my personality was an odd fit for most of the patients there. The clinic's reputation rested on remarkable results, so we charged top dollar. That meant hordes of professional athletes. I coped with my mixed feelings about serving mostly wealthy patients by volunteering my time at a local medical clinic for uninsured patients on occasional weekends.

Liam's case looked to be a clean procedure, but I was nervous. He was the highest profile athlete who'd ever walked through my door, and he made my body do funny things. I wasn't a prudish person. For God's sake, I was a doctor. But I found sex incredibly boring. I didn't have time for relationships and didn't want to make time. Yet, here I had Mr. Sexy-as-hell soccer star sitting in my office and calling me by my first name with that teasing glint in his eyes. I clicked out of the MRI screen and looked up again. I could do this. This weird haywire thing my body was doing would pass.

My eyes collided with Liam's bright blue ones, and my breath hitched. What were we just talking about? Scheduling his surgery. Right.

I swallowed and adjusted my glasses, brushing an errant curl out of the way. "In that case, I'll have them book you for first thing in the morning."

He nodded. "Right then. What time is early for you, luv?"

He was going to have to stop talking. It made me nearly mad that he just called me 'luv' and some part of me, a side I'd never even known existed, liked it. That British accent of his sent flutters twirling in my belly. I could feel my cheeks heating and desperately wished my skin didn't flush at the slightest provocation. "Early is six in the morning. You'll be scheduled for arrival then, and we'll operate by eight." My voice sounded tight, and I prayed he wouldn't notice. He barely knew me, so how could he?

"Perfect. Who's we?"

His eyes held mine in a lazy, teasing look, and I lost track of what I'd just said. "We?" I asked.

"You said 'we' would operate. Aren't you the surgeon?"

"Oh yes, but there will be a team. Myself, the anesthesiologist, a nurse and so on."

One of his dark brows arched up. "I see. I trust you'll be the only one doing whatever it is you'll do to repair my knee."

Once again, I saw a flicker of something other than confidence in his eyes, as when I'd mentioned the tear to him a few minutes earlier. I experienced a pang of sympathy for him, my heart giving a little squeeze. Something about him led me to think he rarely doubted himself, or much of anything. This tiny window into his hidden vulnerability got to me. I suddenly realized I was sitting there staring at him and gave myself a mental shake. *Focus, Olivia. Focus.* I nodded firmly, nudging my mind back into action. "Absolutely. Everyone else is there for support. I'll do the actual surgery part. Maybe we should take some more time to review..."

He shook his head sharply. "I'd rather not hear the details. Just make my knee right. That's all I ask."

His anxiety about his knee was painfully obvious, and it made my heart clench again. It also helped me latch onto a bit of sanity. No one wanted to worry about losing the function of a joint, but a world-class athlete, well, that took worry to an entirely new level. "I meant what I said earlier—the tear isn't bad. I'm confident you'll be good as new once your recovery is complete. You'll need to follow a strict regimen of physical therapy and..."

Liam's grin returned, it's force so powerful, my pulse lunged. "Olivia," he began, his tone holding a hint of haughty, just enough to make my belly do a slow flip. "I'll do absolutely everything you tell me. Not to worry about that."

I literally had to bite the inside of my cheeks to keep from smiling. Flustered beyond belief, I spun around on my stool and pulled up my email on the laptop, firing off an email to Jane who handled all of my surgery scheduling. A prickle ran up my spine, and I knew without looking that Liam had stood and stepped in my direction.

I spun again to find him taking another step. If he was in any pain at the moment, he didn't show it although he took only one step before resting his weight on his good leg. Even with a streak of dirt on his cheek and a temporarily injured knee, Liam Reed was the definition of pure, raw sexy. His body was a work of art. I'd never thought about it much, but right now I realized I had a strong preference for the build of a soccer player. He was lanky and muscled and moved with grace and economy. When I'd received the hurried call from the Seattle Stars office with the news one of their high-profile British players was on the way here, I'd quickly looked up Liam. I didn't search anything other than his sports bio because that's all I wanted to know.

He was considered one of the best midfielders in the world. He'd led his last team in Britain to the league champi-onship in his first year. Seattle news had been filled with reports about the grab the Seattle Stars soccer team had made to snatch Liam and three other players from England at once. I was used to athletes, but Liam was about as high profile as it got around Seattle. I'd had to suffer through a mini-lecture from his team doctor before I came in to meet Liam. I suddenly realized I was staring at him. I was close to level with his face from where I was sitting on the stool. Before I realized what was happening, Liam reached a hand out and gripped the edge of my seat, rolling me toward him, the damned wheels of the stool quite oblivious to my internal resistance.

I was suddenly mere inches away from him, and I

couldn't seem to catch my breath. He emanated an easy strength, so inherent to him it was almost unnoticeable save for the depth of its power. His eyes searched my face, while I seemed to be frozen. Under usual circumstances, if a patient got this close to me, I'd quickly back away. Yet, everything about Liam threw me off kilter. My heart was beating wildly and my cheeks heated again. Before I realized what I was doing, I reached up to adjust my glasses, a nervous habit I'd never managed to break.

"I love your glasses," Liam said, his crisp words falling into the quiet.

Unable to speak, I simply nodded. He angled his head to the side. "I think I'm not supposed to do this, but damn if I can help myself."

While my mind was spinning wildly over what 'this' was, he reached over and removed my glasses. He set them carefully on the counter beside us. I swallowed and tried to rein in my pulse. I wanted to cross my arms and create some kind of barrier against the vulnerable feeling welling inside me. It's not like I could actually hide behind my glasses, but they were a layer and now they were gone. A curl that had been tangled around the temple of my glasses sprung free and bounced against my cheek. He spun the curl around his index finger, a smile playing at the corners of his mouth. My heart was pounding so hard and fast, I was surprised I didn't topple over from the reverberation in my body.

I couldn't look away from Liam's eyes. Fire spread through my veins and the air fairly snapped under the force surrounding us. What the hell was going on? I needed to break out of this moment and now, but I couldn't. All I could see was the blur of Liam's bright blue gaze and the hint of mischief in his eyes, while I had to squeeze my knees together to quell the throb there.

He pulled my curl out, stretching it and then letting it loose where it bounced on my cheek again. "Olivia," he said, almost thoughtfully.

Suddenly, I managed to latch onto some sanity and grabbed the side of the counter and pushed back, the wheels of my stool rolling me back swiftly. "What are you doing?" My voice sounded screechy. I hated it when I sounded like that. I was flustered and flushed—hot inside and out. I abhorred feeling out of control like this and certainly wasn't accustomed to it.

Liam appeared unperturbed and lifted one shoulder in a shrug. "I wanted to see what you tasted like."

If I'd thought I was hot before, I had no idea what hot was. While I should've been thinking he was crazy, I was wondering what he would taste like, even worse I was wondering just what it would be to be tasted by him. Sweet hell. This man made me crazy.

"You can't..." I started to speak and ended up shaking my head wildly.

"Why not? I want you. You're not so sure you want me, but you're curious. You're definitely curious, my dear Olivia." His mouth curled on the corner, a dimple appearing.

I tore my eyes away because it was becoming downright dangerous to look at him. "I can't...we can't do anything like that. I'm your doctor and I'm about to perform surgery on your knee. You can't... you have to stop this."

I could feel his shrug, although I'd turned my back to him. My eyes landed on my glasses on the counter, and I reached over to slip them on.

"We're two consenting adults. If that's the only thing holding you back, let's make a deal. We'll wait until after the surgery."

I didn't like how out of control I felt, not one bit. Annoyed, I spun back around. "*We* aren't waiting to do anything. If you think I'm going to just leap into your arms because you're some kind of soccer god..."

A flash of irritation passed over his face. "Football. It's football."

I waved a hand dismissively, latching onto my annoyance

at feeling out of control. "You know what I mean. Anyway, I'm sure you're used to women falling all over themselves for you, but that's not me. I don't do this. Honestly, sex bores me to tears. I'm sure you think I'm some kind of novelty, but it's not worth your bother. Let me do what I do best and get you back to playing. This, whatever this is you're doing, needs to stop."

The teasing look in his eyes had faded, and he looked genuinely startled. Good. He needed to back the hell off. I could get my stupid body under control, but it would be much better if he'd keep his hands to himself.

"You think sex is boring?" he asked, his tone incredulous.

I didn't even try not to roll my eyes. "Downside to being a doctor, at least for me. I see bodies all the times, including plenty of men in just as good a shape as you." I conveniently omitted the fact it was a miracle I hadn't literally swooned at his feet a few minutes ago. "Sex is for the purpose of procreation, nothing more. I've tried it and found it wanting," I said dismissively. I meant every word I said, yet the moment the words left my mouth, I wondered what it would feel like to experience sex with Liam. All he'd done was exist in the same room with me—injured and clearly not up to par for his usual state—and he'd made me feel things I'd never felt. I could *not* go there.

Liam's eyes widened as I spoke. He shook his head wonderingly. As I sat there in the silence, my belly did another slow flip at the look in his eyes.

"You've just guaranteed I won't be dropping this, luv," he said, that subtle hint of haughty in his tone doing funny things to my insides again.

My mouth went dry at the look in his eyes, and I could feel the wetness between my thighs. I swallowed. "What, what do you mean?"

"You can't go through the rest of your life thinking sex is boring. We'll have to remedy that."

For an injured man, he moved like lightning. He snaked

his arm out and grabbed onto the stool again. In a flash, I was inches away from him, my heart beating so hard, I was afraid he could hear it.

"Maybe we're not supposed to do this, but this will give you something to think about until after my surgery."

He brushed that wild curl off my cheek and dipped his head. His lips came against mine, and electricity jolted through me so hard and fast, I gasped. Holy hell could he kiss. He took his sweet time, dusting my lips with soft kisses, nipping my bottom lip, slipping his tongue inside on a breath. Somewhere along the way, his hand tangled in my hair and he stepped in between my knees. His body was all hard planes and strength. I could feel the ridge of his arousal against me and moaned into his mouth when he nudged his hips into mine. A spike of pleasure shot through me at the subtle point of contact. I wanted more. Now. But he didn't give it to me. He held still and just kept on kissing me. The glide of his tongue against mine made me delirious. I didn't realize I'd slipped a hand up along his chest, savoring the feel of the muscled planes, while I arched into him, desperate for more. Until he slowed his kiss, easing away. He lifted his head, and I was suddenly horrified.

I'd just kissed one of my patients, right here, right now in my examination room. On a scale of one to ten for how horrible this was as far as my career went, this was a solid ten. My eyes collided with his. He looked as startled as I felt. He gave his head a slight shake before stepping back carefully. Reflexively, I reached out to steady him, aware he needed to be careful of his injured knee.

His shoulders rose and fell with a deep breath. Still holding my gaze, he nodded almost as if to himself. "Well, Olivia," he began, his tone sly. "That should give you something to think about. Don't you dare try to pretend that was boring."

Chapter Three

LIAM

"Bloody hell!" I swore as I tried to reach up and grab a banana off the top of the refrigerator.

I kept forgetting my shoulder was stiff as hell and felt foolish every time I did. With a cup of coffee in my free hand, I turned to set it down, just as Alex walked into the kitchen behind me and snagged the banana, handing it to me without a word. He poured a cup of coffee for himself and plunked down at the kitchen table. Just as we had in London, Alex and I shared a flat here. Correct me, a condo. It was cheaper and easier to rent a place together. I peeled the banana and sat down across from him. He sipped his coffee, while I ate my banana in silence. I was cranky today. It was the day after I'd kissed Olivia, and I was fairly certain I'd lost my mind. Oh, I'd wanted to taste her, just like I said. However, my estimation of what kissing her would feel like was staggeringly off base. I'd thought it would just be a fun kiss.

Fun didn't quite capture how it felt to kiss the lovely Olivia. Scalding hot and mind-bending was more like it. Something about her hit me in a strange way. The moment she'd said sex was boring, it was as if she'd poured gas on a fire. I loved a challenge and I'd be damned if I'd let Olivia pass me by. All on her own she was a challenge, but she'd thrown down the gauntlet with that. There was nothing I liked more than a challenge. Then, I'd gone and kissed her. I'd kept it together and managed to tease her afterwards, but I felt as if I'd been knocked back on my heels ever since.

Honestly, I'd felt knocked back on my heels since my mum died. It had been three months now and I didn't know when I'd feel right again. My family was tight. We always had been. I was the oldest of three boys. Mum called us stair steps with me oldest at thirty, Carter at twenty-eight and Leo at twenty-six. My dad was still alive and kicking, but he'd been hit hard by my mum's death too. My parents had met in grammar school and he'd teased her mercilessly, so she hated him. Then, they ended up at university together and fell mad in love. Her stroke had been like a bolt of lightning in our family. I was still reverberating from the electrifying shock.

The one thing that gave me solace was playing football, so I'd insisted on playing in the next few games back in England. I'd pulled through until the last game when I was just plain out of it. I missed a few crucial passes and we lost. Next thing I knew, my agent notified me of the best offer on the table from the Seattle Stars. I glanced over at Alex who turned away from the windows and caught my eye.

"How's the knee?" Alex asked.

His question annoyed me, but only because it reminded me of my current state. Sidelined from playing for a few months at best.

"A bit better than yesterday."

He nodded slowly. "Dr. Bowen seems nice enough."

The feel of Olivia's lips under mine flashed through my brain. Nice was one way to put it. "That she does. Dr. Monroe swears she's the best surgeon around."

Alex grinned. "He had his knickers in a bit of a twist over her asking him to leave. I told him to roll with it."

I couldn't help but chuckle. Since we'd only been with the Stars for a little over a month, I was still getting a feel for the team management. Dr. Monroe was wound tight and struck me as the kind of man accustomed to people following his orders. Olivia hadn't given a damn about his orders, and I liked it. "I could tell. I think he thought she'd cave when he got pushy, but she didn't."

Alex's gaze sobered. "Anything new from her when you talked?"

"Nah. She said the tear's not too bad and seems confident I'll be back to myself in a few months. She's as bossy as him. Gave me a little lecture on doing my physical therapy after my surgery," I said with a grin.

Alex finished off his coffee and winked. "Not so sure it's a brilliant plan to flirt with your doctor, mate."

I'd been born a flirt and Alex damn well knew it. I eyed him and shrugged. "You know me. Can't help myself sometimes."

Alex stood and stretched before walking to the sink and setting his empty coffee cup inside. He had practice in a bit, which sent anxiety coiling inside my chest. I hated not being able to play. I wished my surgery were today, so I could be one day ahead in getting back to playing. Football anchored my life and kept me sane. Without it, I was restless and out of sorts.

Alex turned, crossing his arms and leaning against the counter. "Maybe you can't help yourself, but Dr. Bowen doesn't strike me as your type. Let her do what she does best and fix your knee. You've plenty of women falling over themselves for you. It's worse here than it was in London," he said with a roll of his eyes.

"I'll bloody well decide who I'm going to flirt with. You're the one who should be enjoying the women here."

I couldn't help but feel a tad bit churlish. Alex knew me

well, as well as anyone did. He might not specifically know I'd gone a step further than flirting with Olivia. He also might not specifically know I was gobsmacked over her. Yet, he'd know something was amiss with me. Hence, my churlishness. Alex was my best mate, but it didn't mean I always appreciated how well he knew me. I preferred to feel in control, and everything about my life lately led to the opposite between my mum dying, moving to Seattle, and now having my knee blown. What I'd expected to be a moment when I was in control turned out to be the opposite. That kiss with Olivia had, well, it had blown my mind. All I wanted was more.

Chapter Four

OLIVIA

I tugged the front of my raincoat together and dashed through the heavy drizzle. Once I was across the street, I pushed through the swinging door into Desert Isle Café. I flung my hood back and gave my coat a shake before glancing around. My glasses immediately fogged from the contrasting warm air, creating a blurry halo. Removing them, I dried them on the bottom of my shirt and slipped them back on. The scent of baked goods and coffee assailed me.

"Olivia, over here!"

I looked around to see my best friend Daisy Knight waving from a table in the corner. I returned her wave and headed for the counter. I was cold straight through from my walk here and needed coffee to warm me up. Moments later, I threaded through the tables in the crowded coffee shop and slipped into the chair across from Daisy. I'd known Daisy since we were in first grade. She glanced up from whatever she was doing on her laptop and grinned, her smile wide and welcoming. Daisy was like her name—cheery and warm with a whimsical side. With her blonde hair, dark brown eyes and curvaceous figure, she was plain gorgeous and also one of the kindest people I knew. Daisy and I had gone to medical school together, although she'd gone into medical research, while I'd gone into surgery. No matter how busy we were, we had a standing coffee date every week. Desert Isle Café was our favorite place for coffee, named as a shake of the fist to Seattle's rainy weather and a metaphorical oasis on a rainy day.

Daisy saved whatever she was working on and closed her laptop, sliding it into its padded shoulder bag, before turning her gaze to me. "Hey, hey, what's up?"

I curled my hands around the steaming hot mug of coffee, sighing at the warmth. "Aside from the fact I'm freezing, nothing new."

Daisy took a sip of her own coffee, her perceptive brown gaze coasting over me. "Let me guess, you didn't bother to check the weather and wore just your scrubs. Thank God, I don't have to wear those everyday for research."

I laughed softly. Daisy knew me well. I worked long hours and rarely bothered to manage the logistics of my life. "There's never anything new with me," I countered with a roll of my eyes. The moment the words left my mouth, I thought of Liam's kiss yesterday and heat raced up my cheeks.

Daisy cocked her head to the side. "What are you blushing about?"

I took a gulp of my coffee and glared at her. "Nothing."

She shrugged. I breathed an internal sigh of relief, thinking she was going to drop it. I should've known better. Daisy had an unerring ability to know what might be getting under my skin.

"What's this I hear about Liam Reed? Sports news says you're in charge of fixing his blown knee," Daisy said with a sly smile.

I leaned back in my chair and fought to keep my face from turning even redder. "You've got to be kidding me! Is that actually news?"

"Of course it's news. He's a hot soccer star from Britain. He's not just famous here hon, but everywhere." She must've taken a tiny bit of pity on me at the look on my face and shook her head slowly. "I heard about it on the sports radio on the way into work this morning. The radio guys spent like twenty minutes discussing his injury. I'll never understand why some guy who plays ball gets more time on the news than things like poverty, but hey, that's our world. Anyway, they said he'd been assigned to Dr. Bowen at your clinic. Pretty sure that's you."

I took another gulp of coffee followed with a deep breath. Usually I didn't even think about the pressure of operating on athletes, but the way Liam rattled me was shaking my composure at all levels. "Obviously it's me. It's not like I can talk about it," I mumbled, knowing perfectly well the clinic had already obtained a full disclosure for Liam and the team. That's how it worked there. If famous sports stars wanted their potentially career-ending injuries turned around under the scalpel of any surgeon at the clinic, they had to be willing to sign releases for updates on their recovery. I rarely discussed anything, except in cases when I was asked to make public statements about recovery times and whatnot.

Daisy was quite aware of this as well and merely rolled her eyes. "I don't give a damn about his knee. I'm just wondering how come you can't stop blushing."

If anyone could keep me from losing my mind over Liam, it would be Daisy. She was my dearest friend, the only friend I had who'd been there before my parents died. When I was ten years old, my parents died together in a car accident on their way to a holiday party. To this day, I hated the holidays. My mom's twin sister Lorraine had raised me after that. She was loving and kind, but she'd been as lost as I had been after my parents died. She and my mother had been quite close as twins. Lorraine lived in the small town Daisy and I grew up in a short drive outside of Seattle. Aside from Daisy and a few other friends, she was really the only other person in my life whom I stayed close with. I was what most people called an introvert. I didn't know if I'd been that way before my parents died. Daisy insisted I'd been a bit less standoff-ish. Either way, getting close to people wasn't the easiest thing for me.

I looked over at Daisy and blushed even deeper at the twinkle in her eyes. "I'm blushing because Liam Reed seems to think he can make a move on me. I don't know what the hell to do about it," I blurted out.

Daisy's eyes widened, and I experienced a flash of satis-faction at actually startling her. She quickly recovered and grinned. "Well, it's about damn time. You are flat out gorgeous. I'd bet plenty of your patients want to get in your pants. Nice to know the hottest ticket in town has the sense to notice how amazing you are."

I put my hands on my cheeks, as if I could somehow cool the heat. "Are you insane?!"

Daisy shrugged. "Definitely not. He'll do great things for your career. Make his knee good as new and then screw his brains out. Maybe you'll have fun for once in your life."

I stared at her, torn between the warring factions inside of me. There was the usual side of me that wanted to tell her she was seriously out of her mind. Then, there was this new, foreign side that thought screwing Liam's brains out might be the best thing I ever did. Just the thought of it sent heat scoring through my center and a throb in my channel. *Sex is boring. Remember? It's not like you haven't tried it before. Maybe so, but not with Liam. One kiss from him was all kinds of amazing.* If I could have slapped the voice inside my head, I would've. This was madness, plain and simple. I latched onto the part of me I knew better.

"I don't need to have fun. Most certainly not with a high-profile patient," I said defensively.

Daisy rolled her eyes. "You need to loosen up is what you need. I've seen his photos. Liam Reed is all kinds of sexy.

Most women would get off just seeing him naked. As for him being your patient...after the surgery, hon," she said with a sly wink.

I balled up a napkin and threw it at her where it bounced off her shoulder and landed on the table between us. "Would you stop it?! It's crazy and you know it. Plus, you know how I feel about sex. I'd bet sex with an arrogant sports star is about as boring as it gets."

I was rewarded with another eye roll from Daisy. "It's not like you gave it much of a shot. You dated what, maybe three guys in college? You should try again."

Daisy was the opposite of me when it came to dating. She was on the hunt for the perfect guy and wasn't the least bit shy about it. I knew behind her bravado there was a soft side and a warm heart, so sometimes I worried about her boldness. Mostly, it puzzled me because I sincerely had found sex to be boring, boring enough I hadn't thought it worth the effort to cast around. Maybe it was a stroke of bad, boring luck for me. They weren't bad guys, just nothing revved my engine. I held Daisy's gaze and shrugged. "Don't really have time and you know it."

Daisy shook her head. At that moment, the bell jingled above the door to the café. Reflexively, I glanced over and my pulse took off. Liam walked through the door with the man who'd been in the waiting room with him yesterday. I barely noticed the guy with my eyes nearly devouring Liam. Liam's dark hair was damp from the rain. He hadn't bothered with a raincoat, and his slightly damp, long-sleeved t-shirt clung to his muscled shoulders. I didn't know how it was possible, but even with a subtle limp, the man was so damn sexy he took my breath away. He turned, his eyes catching mine from across the room and sending flutters in a spin through my belly.

Daisy's giggle had me tearing my eyes off of him. I turned back to her. If I thought I'd blushed before, now it was worse, way worse. I felt like I was on fire inside and out.

Chapter Five

LIAM

The moment I stepped into the coffee shop, I knew Olivia was there. A prickle raced up my spine. I ran a hand over my damp hair and turned slowly, finding her in the corner at a table with another woman. Olivia's eyes locked to mine for a flash. Even from across the busy room, I could feel her presence. It was as if a flame licked its way through the air across the room. She tore her eyes free the moment I started to smile. Bloody hell, that woman set a storm brewing inside me.

Alex nudged my shoulder. "Move it, mate. You're staring."

I glanced his way and met his knowing gaze. With a shrug, I made my way to the counter behind him. Alex had dragged me here this morning after practice was cut short due to the rain. The team often practiced inside as it was, yet Coach sent everyone home to study tapes. Coach Bernie had ordered me to observe practice today and given me hell for skipping the day prior. I'd protested that I was scheduled for surgery tomorrow morning, but he'd merely locked his sharp blue gaze on me and arched a brow. He didn't expect me to actually practice, but he fully expected me to watch from the sidelines and participate in planning with the team.

Despite my disgruntled state about being shipped clear across the pond to the US and all the way to its West Coast, I liked Coach Bernie. In fact, in the short time I'd been playing under him, he'd become my favorite coach. He was sharp as a tack and tough, but not a bloody arse. The man was rock solid confident without a drop of arrogance. I respected the hell out of him. Bernard Hoffman had been a hella footballer back in his heyday roughly fifteen years ago. He'd retired after sustaining far too many injuries in a car accident, an accident that killed his wife. He'd yet to speak a word to me about my mum, but I sensed he knew the loss was affecting me and understood it better than most. Unlike some coaches, I knew he wouldn't push me to play too soon after my injury, but he'd bloody well expect me to be active on the sidelines and be studying tapes like a madman until I was back in action.

After Coach set us free a bit ago, Alex insisted he needed coffee before we trudged through the rain to spend an after-noon watching tapes. London was famous for its dreary weather, yet I was fairly certain Seattle had it beat. If it wasn't raining a slow drizzle most days, the sky was usually overcast. I looked around while we waited for our coffees and ignored the two women trying to flirt with us. Alex was the master at ignoring flirts. He simply leaned a shoulder against the wall, slipped his hands in his pockets and stayed quiet. I wasn't accustomed to wanting to ignore a little fun banter. I'd freely admit I considered it a bonus perk of being a famous footballer—woman all over the world knew who I was and lavished attention on me. Yet right now, it made me restless and annoyed. I resorted to pulling my phone out of my pocket and staring aimlessly at it. All the while, I beat back the urge to walk over and say hello to Olivia.

When our names were called, Alex snagged our coffees and returned to my side. His eyes flicked from me past my shoulder where Olivia was sitting. "Alright mate, you'd best say hi to your doctor. Won't do to ignore her," he said with a wink.

I slipped my phone in my pocket and took the cup of coffee he held out, refusing to be baited by his wink. A gulp and then I nodded. "Right then."

A few steps later, I stopped beside Olivia. Those bright green eyes of hers landed on mine, and awareness sliced through me. Rather than the usual subtle thrill I got from being drawn to a woman, the two times I'd gotten near Olivia, the pull was so strong it startled me. It wasn't a simple thrill, it was pure, raw need. She adjusted her glasses with a tight smile. "Hello, Liam."

Over the pounding of my heart, I managed a nod and scrambled to grab hold of my usual smooth banter. "Nice to see you, luv...once before I go under your knife." There. My teasing habits helped. Her cheeks flushed rosy red, and all I wanted was to kiss her.

The woman with Olivia smiled brightly, her eyes bouncing from Alex to me. "Well, it's the Brit boys playing for Seattle. So nice to meet you two."

I managed to tear my eyes away from Olivia. The woman across from her would normally have caught my attention, what with her blonde hair tied back in a sleek knot, her wide brown eyes and a curvy little body sheathed in a fitted blouse and skirt. Yet, I might as well have been staring at a blank wall for all my body noticed her. Alex, who hated the attention that came with being a world-class footballer, flushed just the slightest bit. If I hadn't known him my whole life, I probably wouldn't have noticed. He shifted his shoulders and took a swallow of coffee. When the woman with Olivia arched a brow, I realized neither one of us had bothered to reply. "Right you are. Liam Reed," I said with a practiced flourish and a nod. "This here is Alex Gordon. He rarely speaks, but he plays like a dream." That was my usual intro to Alex, which tended to annoy him enough he stopped being silent.

He nodded. "Alex," he said gruffly. His eyes flicked to Olivia. "Dr. Bowen, you'll take good care of my best mate's knee tomorrow, right?"

Olivia looked to Alex. "Of course!" She looked startled by his comment.

"Of course she will! Olivia's the best orthopedic surgeon you'll find," her friend said firmly.

Olivia flushed again and rolled her eyes. "I do my best," she said softly. She glanced between Alex and I and gestured to the woman across from her. "This is Daisy Knight. She's a good friend of mine."

"We're besties," Daisy said with a grin.

I managed to participate in the next few minutes of conversation like a semi-normal person, while inside I was thrown off. Olivia's presence seemed to have a disconcerting power over me. That combined with Alex's comment about my pending surgery had knocked me sideways. I'd been doing my damnedest to keep my mind off my knee. It would be fine. Olivia said so. I shoved those thoughts away and tried to focus on her. Ever since she'd said sex was boring, I'd been contemplating just how amazing it would be with her. Because I would have her. One way or another. No matter how much it threw me to be near her, I couldn't turn down a challenge, not one that I suspected would lead to the best sex of my life.

I hadn't realized I'd zoned out when Daisy said something that caught my attention. "You mean to tell me you boys haven't gone to the Space Needle yet? That's it, after Olivia works her magic on your knee, we're going."

Alex shifted his weight on his feet, and I knew quite well he was thinking he'd rather not. I didn't give a damn. Any chance to socialize with Olivia was a firm yes for me. "Bloody perfect. We'd love to go," I said.

I glanced to Alex to see him shift his shoulders uncomfortably. He didn't do things like this often. "We need to see more of Seattle. All we've seen so far is downtown and our stadium." I looked to Olivia to see her fiddling with a napkin. Her dark hair seemed a bit curlier than it had the other day, likely due to the damp rain. A few curls were poking out of the knot atop her head like wild children. One wound around the temple of her glasses, and I itched to reach over and free it.

Her eyes canted up and collided with mine. I felt as if I'd been punched in the chest, that's how hard the force of her gaze hit me. Daisy was saying something and I didn't hear a damn thing. Alex nudged my shoulder, and I managed to look back at Daisy. Her wide brown eyes held a gleam. I sensed she knew perfectly well I was gobsmacked over her friend, but she was kind enough not to tease. "Best of luck with your surgery tomorrow," she said. "If you're worried, you don't need to be. Olivia truly is one of the best. You'll be back on the field before you know it."

I fervently hoped she was right. I had faith in Olivia, but the vagaries of recovering from an injury in sports were well known. That anxiety I'd been trying to beat back started to rear its head again, so I forced myself to talk, anything other than thinking. "I'd say I'll do my best, but I'll not be doing much more than lying there. Here's hoping," I returned with a lift of my paper coffee cup. Obviously, I'd missed a few steps in the conversation. Alex nodded to Daisy and Olivia. "We'd best be going." His eyes locked onto Olivia's. "I'll see you in the morning."

"Oh, you'll be with Liam?" she asked.

"Of course," he said gruffly. "Someone's got to make sure he's on time," he added with a sly grin, masking his concern. Alex was my best mate in every sense. He was the one who wouldn't even think of going about his day without making sure he was there for the start and finish of my surgery. My chest tightened a little. I'd been a bit of an emotional pansy since my mum had died and moments like this brought it out.

My familiar defense of teasing helped me get through the next few minutes. I winked at Daisy and locked eyes with Olivia. "Alright, luv. I expect you to live up to your reputation tomorrow."

Her cheeks flushed, and my cock got hard. That's it. All she had to do was flush, and it was like a bolt of lightning inside me. "I'll see you in the morning," she said with another slight smile.

The only reason I managed to leave was Alex nudging my shoulder and walking alongside me on the way out. I ignored the rain as we walked home, my mind bouncing between the disconcerting anxiety about my knee and what could happen to my career if I didn't recover fully, and thoughts of Olivia. Her bright green eyes, her lush lips and her dark curls. I wanted to see her hair loose with a ferocity that bordered on madness.

Chapter Six

OLIVIA

I stood in the break room, the surgery clinic's equivalent of a locker room, and stared into the mirror in my locker. My hair was an unruly mess. Curls had escaped from their knot and were pointing every which way. I quickly untied it and grabbed a brush. A few minutes later, I had the wild locks tamed and tied up in their usual knot. My hair didn't suit my career. Nothing but a tight knot kept it halfway controlled. In a ponytail, my curls behaved like Medusa. Loose, they were pure madness. When I was operating, I needed nothing in my way, certainly not errant curls getting in my eyes. I occasionally considered cutting it short, but for reasons I didn't quite understand, I couldn't bring myself to do so. My mind skipped back a few days to when Liam wrapped one of my curls around his finger. Heat spun in my center. I turned from the mirror and quickly changed out of my surgical uniform.

Liam's surgery had gone as smoothly as I'd expected. After a clean repair, I expected him to be back on track to play within three months. I had tried not to think much about the surgery this morning. I was usually calm and unruffled by high pressure surgeries. Yet, Liam made me nervous. Well, maybe not Liam, more my own reaction to him. I wasn't supposed to worry about the weight of expectations and rarely did. In Liam's case, what kept spinning through my mind was the flicker of fear deep in his eyes when I'd spoken about his surgery the day I met him. His career was central to his life, as it was to most professional athletes. With him, it felt as if I'd be personally letting him down if I didn't live up to the trust he'd placed in me to make his knee right again.

Then, there was the way he looked at me. Oh, and the fact he kissed me and I could hardly stop thinking about it. In fact, I'd had a few hot and bothered fantasies about those strong hands of his all over my body. Just now, here in the sterile break room that doubled as a changing room for surgeons and where anyone could walk in, I flushed straight through. I could feel the slick heat between my thighs and took a shaky breath. The effect Liam had on me was getting ridiculous. I wished he hadn't kissed me. Better yet, I wished I'd had the will to shove him away. As it was, I hadn't. All I could do was be grateful I'd managed to keep my cool and operate as I always did. Now came the hard part. I needed to check on him in the recovery room and have a few follow up appointments over the next few weeks. Once those were done, I could turn him over to the nursing and physical therapy team.

I was rattled by how much I wanted him. It was all made worse by the fact that I'd never been this attracted to anyone. I'd been so confident in my ability *not* to be affected by men that I felt like a fool. All Liam had to do was exist in my presence, and my body was electrified with heat and need. With a mental shake, I tugged on a clean set of scrubs and walked down the hall toward the recovery room. Our facility offered private recovery rooms for all patients, a perk most clinics didn't provide. As I got closer to the door to Liam's room, my pulse picked up and heat spun inside. This was beyond ridiculous. I was checking on a patient. It was completely inappropriate to be thinking or feeling anything about him. My body had other ideas.

I entered the room to find Liam's friend Alex slouched in a chair by the bed. He looked up, his brown hair mussed. For the first time, I noticed how he looked. Like Liam, he had a body of pure muscle. He was taller and exuded a powerful sense of quiet. I knew from Daisy that Alex was considered one of the best goalkeepers in the world. I could see why, not because I'd ever seen him play, but more because of the sense of calm alertness he gave off. I doubted he ever lost focus. He stood and gave his shoulders a shake as he rounded the foot of the bed.

I met him there and quickly tapped the screen at the foot of the bed, which contained the data from Liam's vitals in the hour since the surgery. "Everything looks good," I said, keeping my voice low.

I looked up into Alex's brown eyes to see him nodding. "Good then," he said.

"Bloody hell. You two don't have to whisper."

Alex and I swung in unison to look toward Liam. He looked groggy, as he should, but he was definitely awake. Reflexively, I stepped to the side of the bed, resting a hand on his hip. Alex went to the other side of the bed and looked down at Liam.

"How are you feeling?" I asked.

"Thirsty," Liam replied. Even groggy from surgery, he managed a slight grin.

I turned to the table by his bed and quickly poured a small cup of water. As he took it from me, a phone rang. Well, it didn't actually ring. A song erupted—to be specific, the Beatles, All You Need is Love. Liam's weak grin expanded.

Alex muttered something and yanked his phone out. "It's Dr. Monroe," he said, flicking his eyes from the screen to Liam and I. "He'll be expecting an update."

"Go ahead and tell him the surgery went well, and I'll call him later," I replied.

Alex nodded and turned away to answer the phone, stepping to the windows as he did. I glanced down at Liam. "I suspect he'll want to stop by. He called this morning requesting to come by before your prep. I turned him away."

Liam's eyes widened. He gulped the remainder of water in the cup I'd handed him and set it on the bed. I reached to move it to the table, but he caught my hand in his and gave it a squeeze. "I bloody love how bossy you are."

I flushed and tried to distract myself with a stern look at him. "Now is not the time to flirt, Liam." Desperate to distract myself from how easily he affected me, I collected my thoughts and focused on the practical matters. "Aside from thirsty, how are you feeling?"

"Fuzzy. Not a bit of pain, not even a wee bit. I suppose this nice woozy feeling will pass though."

"Soon enough. You shouldn't have too much pain though. Like I said, the tear wasn't too bad. You'll have some soreness and then you'll need to take it easy for a few days before you start physical therapy."

For a flash, uncertainty flickered in the back of Liam's bright blue eyes. This man—this cocky, swoon-worthy man who'd spun me in circles inside and kissed me senseless—elicited a sudden pang of empathy from me. I could only guess at how frightening this experience must be for him. It wasn't about the pain. A meniscus tear was by no means a life-threatening medical issue, yet for a man whose life was built on his physical prowess and athletic skill, well, it held the potential to thwart his entire career.

I didn't realize I gave his hand a squeeze until I felt him squeeze in return. At that moment, Alex turned back from the windows. "Dr. Monroe said he's coming by and he doesn't give a damn if you want him to wait," Alex said, his eyes on me.

I slipped my hand free from Liam's, suddenly aware of

just how unprofessional it was to be squeezing his hand. Wishing I wasn't so prone to blushing, I swallowed and nodded. Normally, I'd be flat annoyed with Dr. Monroe, but I was off kilter due to Liam's effect on me. I looked down to Liam. "Is that okay with you? If not..."

"Don't you worry. I can handle Dr. Monroe," Liam said, his tone cheeky.

How a man who was half out of it from anesthesia managed to be cheeky, I didn't know. I rolled my eyes and shook my head. "Fine then. I'll stay with him while he's here."

Alex rested his hip on the far side of the bed. "I like you, Dr. Bowen," he announced suddenly.

Puzzled at his comment, I looked over at him. Before I spoke, he continued. "You're making sure Liam comes first, not the team. That's why." He glanced to Liam. "You need to stop teasing her, mate. She's your doctor," he said, his voice somber. His intent gaze swung back to me. "Don't mind him, he can't help himself sometimes."

Liam leaned his head back against the pillows and sighed mightily. "Alex acts like my mum sometimes. That's why he's my best mate," he said matter-of-factly.

At that, his eyes closed, and he promptly fell asleep.

I looked across at Alex and wondered if he sensed I was tossed asunder inside. Here I was, completely accustomed to keeping my cool at all times around athletes of all stripes, and I all in a twitter inside over Liam. I wondered if Alex's warning was as much for me as Liam.

Chapter Seven

LIAM

I looked over at Coach and fought the urge to roll my eyes. His steely gaze met mine. "You'll be here every other practice to observe and meet with the team and that's final," Coach said firmly.

It had been a full two weeks since my surgery, and I was bored with sitting on the sidelines at practices. Coach didn't appear to give a damn. One of the things I liked about him was his absolute commitment to a team mindset. Right about now, that commitment meant he expected me to drag my sorry arse here every other day since I was part of the team.

"You're not just a player on this team, you're a leader. Act like it," Coach said, his words hitting me right in my chest.

I swallowed against the tight feeling in my throat. I didn't like thinking about how much this bloody knee injury had shaken my confidence. I hadn't helped lead my last team to a championship by questioning myself. It was brutal to watch the team practice and watch hours of practice tapes, knowing I wouldn't be back in play for another two months at best. Coach's confidence in me, and faith I'd have a full recovery was hard to accept. I took a breath and met his gaze with a nod. I'd fake it to make it if I had to.

Coach leaned back in his chair and picked up a snow globe on his desk. He idly turned it in his hands. He was so damn perceptive, it made me want to squirm in my seat, so I was relieved to have him look away finally. I flexed and straightened my knee slightly, noticing the soreness was minimal.

Coach's voice startled me. "We haven't spoken of it, but I'm sorry about your mother."

What the hell? I had no idea why Coach chose now to mention my mum. Rubbing salt in the wound was how it felt. I was stumbling, literally and figuratively, around these days, and he had to go and pick now to talk about her. My heart gave a painfully hard thump, and my throat tightened again. I missed her. So damn much. I closed my eyes and blinked back the hot tears pressing there. Bloody hell. I couldn't cry. Not here. Not now. Not in front of Coach. For once, I honed in on the lingering soreness in my knee. Most of the time, I preferred to pretend it didn't hurt. But right now, that bit of physical pain was preferable to thinking about my mum and the stroke that had stolen her from us. After another moment, I managed to get a handle on myself and opened my eyes.

Coach's gaze was no longer steely, but rather understanding. He was quiet and then nodded, almost as if to himself. "I know a bit about losing someone. I know it worries you that it's affected your concentration. Maybe it has. Can't say because I wasn't your coach before. From what I know of you, you're a good man and you loved your mother—that much is obvious. You can't turn back the clock. All you can do is move forward with your eye on the ball, so to speak. You're a helluva a player. If you have any weakness, it's you don't draw deep because you never had to. Think on that while you've some downtime."

At that, he stood. He didn't speak it aloud, but it was clear he understood I didn't have it in me to respond to him right now. I managed to stand slowly and snagged my crutches on the way down the long hall from his office.

A few hours later, I waited in a chair at Olivia's clinic. I'd been flat out running in my mind ever since Coach had met with me. Confused and casting about for what the hell he'd meant about me needing to 'draw deep,' I'd zoned in on thinking about Olivia. She was a most efficient distraction because she'd been driving me beyond mad. I'd had two appointments with her since the surgery, and she'd been nothing but calm, cool and professional in both despite the air fairly humming with electricity around us. I meant to have her, and I would.

The door to her examining room opened, and another patient exited. Olivia caught my eyes and held a finger up before turning back into the room. She was a bossy one and expected people to follow her orders. I surmised she meant for me to wait, so I didn't. I stood and walked carefully to the examination room. I was using crutches most of the time, but left them leaning up against the wall. It wasn't like they were going anywhere.

When I stepped through the door, Olivia was pulling a fresh sheet of paper from the rollers onto the table. I thanked the stars she hadn't heard me. The rustle of the paper kept her from hearing me quietly close the door. Finally having a moment alone with her sent a lash of lust through me. With her leaning over the table, her delectable bottom was outlined for me. She wore a skirt today, which I liked. Quite a lot. It was a simple fitted skirt that came to her knees, nothing even the slightest bit scandalous about it. But I could imagine shoving it up over her hips and getting a taste of her. She straightened and turned, her eyes widening when she saw me. She wore a white lab coat over her skirt with a blue shirt underneath that stretched tight across her breasts. Oh, it was something to see her out of her scrubs. It wasn't as if she was dressed to impress, it was just that she tempted me beyond all reason. My cock was rock hard and ready, and she hadn't done a thing.

Her cheeks flushed, and she reached up to adjust her glasses and brush a random curl out of her eyes. "Liam..." She started to speak, but trailed off after she said my name. I waited, leashing the urge to step to her, lift her onto the table and slide my hands up her legs. She cleared her throat and gave her head a little shake. "How's the knee feeling?" she asked, her words crisp and clear.

"Right as rain." I closed the distance between us, stopping beside the table where her hip rested against it. "I hear from my PT guy that this is my last appointment with you unless I experience a delay in my recovery." I knew I was standing a tad too close for her comfort, but I wanted to rattle her composure. There was that and this overwhelming need to be as close as possible to her. She was a challenge I wanted to win. I also craved being able to lose myself in the raw need she elicited. It was about the only thing that took my mind off worrying about my professional playing and Coach's out of the blue comments about losing my mum.

I looked down at her and before I knew it, I lifted my hand and trailed a fingertip down her cheek. Her skin was like silk, and the soft flush on her cheeks against her creamy complexion sent a blast of heat through me. She reached up and adjusted her glasses again. Once I'd touched her, I couldn't stop, so my finger trailed down her cheek and along her neck, brushing past the wild flutter of her pulse, which sent a wash of satisfaction through me. "I think we discussed that you didn't have to worry about me being your patient soon," I said, my voice coming out low and gruff.

Olivia's green eyes slammed into mine as she shook her head. "Liam... We didn't... We didn't discuss anything like that. You did, but I didn't. This isn't...I can't..." Her words came in fits and starts, her cheeks flushing deeper by the second.

I knew it bothered her to have me pursuing her, and not only did I not give a damn, but the naughtier she thought it was, the more I wanted her. I also knew, somewhere deep down inside, that the desire between us was like no other, and I had to experience it.

"Olivia, don't go thinking we can't do this because it's not proper. It's perfectly proper. This is my last appointment with you unless I have some complications, so that's no good excuse. Let's get this exam over with, so we can move on." It took every ounce of discipline I had to step back and slide my hips onto the table when I wanted to turn her around, bend her over and sink inside. The only thing that got me through it was knowing the longer I dragged it out, the more she'd want me. It was hard to fathom wanting her more than I already did, but I was bound and determined to make sure she never, ever thought sex with me was boring. That meant this play had to be my A-game all the way and no rushing.

Olivia took a step back and snatched her computer tablet off the counter. I watched while she clicked through screens. The flush on her cheeks eased, while my cock stayed hard and ready. She barely looked my way as she commented that the latest MRI results looked good and asked a few questions about my physical therapy. Then came the good part. She set down the computer tablet and checked my knee, carefully testing the flexion. Even though her touch was impersonal, I loved having her hands on me. She stepped away and finally met my eyes. I winked, and her cheeks went cherry red again.

"Are we all done with that, doc?"

Olivia nodded. "Everything looks good. Unless you have trouble, you should be all set with your physical therapy schedule." Her words came out raspy.

I watched her for a minute before sliding off the table. I'd come to know she liked to stand close when I did that, as if she was concerned I'd land wrong on my knee. She quickly stepped to my side and was there when my feet met the floor. Perfect. I slid my hands around her hips and turned, lifting her onto the table. I wasn't quite sure how I pulled it off, but the angle was just so and I barely had to turn with both of us standing beside the table.

The little squeak that escaped from her lips was like a whip cracking inside me. I was standing between her knees and gave her hips a little tug, just enough that I could feel the heat of her against my cock. As much as I wanted to grind my hips into her, I didn't. I wasn't much for planning when it came to women, but I was when it came to Olivia. I wanted her to want me as badly as I wanted her, and I wanted to show her sex was anything but boring.

I let my eyes travel up her body, savoring the lush curves of her breasts, which were rising and falling with her rapid breath. Given that my heart was all but pounding its way out of my body, I was a bit relieved she was in a similar state. When my gaze met hers, her eyes were snapping.

"Liam, what are you doing?" she asked. It sounded as if she was trying to be stern, but it didn't quite come out that way. Her voice was breathy instead, the sound of it cracking the whip inside me again.

I reached up and removed her glasses. "I thought I'd give you a taste of something."

She bit her lip and damn if that didn't nearly make me lose control and nudge my cock against the heat of her. I clung to the edge of my control—it took all of my strength not to tumble loose into the desire heavy in the air around us.

I set her glasses down on the table beside us and reached up to pull one of those curls. Damn, even her curls made me crazy. She was so tidy and professional. I'd bet she had perfect scores in school and always followed the rules. She was wound so tight that those disobedient curls did something to me. A few had escaped from the tight knot she kept them in. I wound one around my finger and dragged it out before letting it loose where it bounced on her cheek. She was silent, her eyes dark, her pulse fluttering under her skin, and her breath coming in short pants. I gave in and nudged my hips into the cradle of hers, almost groaning aloud at the wet heat I could feel through the thin fabric of her panties. It was splendid that she was wearing a skirt, which had conveniently slid up her hips when I lifted her onto the table.

I gave in and reached one hand down to her ankle, curling around it and sliding up over the bare skin of her leg.

"Liam…" she said on a breath.

I dipped my head and dusted kisses along the side of her neck, savoring the feel of her pulse beating wildly there. "Mmm?" I asked in a mumble against her skin.

I dropped kisses along her collarbone while I slipped my other hand around her hips and pulled her a bit closer. My hand had reached her thigh, and I could feel her trembling. I didn't stop and kept sliding up over the silk of her skin until I reached the hem of her skirt. For a few beats, I paused and then kept going, letting the fabric bunch over my wrist as I reached the juncture of her thighs. With her trembling under my touch and the feel and scent of her surrounding me, it was a damn miracle I didn't tear her clothes off and sink into her right then and there. I had a goal and that goal was nothing short of earth shattering pleasure for her. So no rushing, not even a little.

I dragged my thumb back and forth over her panties, delighted to discover the silk was nearly drenched wet. I dallied there, back and forth, back and forth, coasting over the nub of her desire again and again and again until her hips rolled into my touch. Only then did I lift my head and look at her. I almost lost it. With her cheeks flushed and her eyelids at half-mast, she was so mind-boggling sexy, I could hardly stand it.

"So tell me Olivia...do you want me to stop?" I asked. I never paused in the slow tease of my fingers over the wet silk between her thighs.

Her eyes met mine. She was quiet, the moment so taut and heavy with desire, it took everything I had to wait for her response. She finally shook her head, just the tiniest bit. I trailed my thumb over her clit again, lingering for a second, just long enough that her hips arched into my touch. I had to have more. I hooked a finger over the silk and pushed it out of the way. Holy hell. She was dripping wet. A whimper escaped from her when I slid my fingers into her folds. I looked down and could hardly look away. With her knees spread apart, her skirt bunched up and her bottom pulled to the edge of the table, her pink folds, wet and glistening, stood out against the sterile white paper on the examining table.

I slid a finger into her channel and groaned at the feel of her clenching around me. I tore my eyes away and looked up. I was going to make her come—right here, right now—and watch every second of her pleasure. She was close, already so close, and I could tell. "Does that feel good?" I asked.

She moaned and nodded jerkily when I slid another finger inside. Her hips were rolling into my touch as I began to stroke in and out of her channel. Her knees fell further apart, and her breath came in heaving gasps. Her body went taut, her channel throbbing around my fingers. For all that was holy, she nearly brought me to my knees.

"Olivia," I said.

Her eyes came open slowly.

"Come here," I ordered as I slid my palm up her spine, exerting a subtle pressure to bring her to me. I needed to have her lips under mine when she came. I had to feel the pleasure in her kiss.

I kept up the pace with my fingers as she leaned forward. I caught her lips just as I swirled my thumb around her swollen clit. She cried out into our kiss, her channel convulsing around my fingers. I eased away from her mouth and looked down between us. My proper Dr. Bowen had her knees wide with my fingers buried inside of her. A part of me savored the thrill of conquering this layer of her resistance, while another part of me was half-stunned at how it felt to be with her like this. There was a connection with her—burning incandescent and so hot it nearly scalded me.

I looked to her face to find her eyes, those gorgeous green eyes, looking back at me. She looked beyond surprised, but the usual lines of tension were gone from her face. Latching onto something to keep me from wondering just what it was about her that hit me so hard, I went to the familiar. "So, Olivia, was that boring?"

She rewarded me by narrowing her eyes and glaring at me. "No," she replied, her tone slightly defensive.

There was a knock on the door, and I was thankful for thinking ahead. I'd had the sense to lock the door when I stepped into the room. Olivia didn't know that though and scrambled back, nearly kicking me out of the way. "Easy, luv. I locked the door." I placed a hand on her hip to hold her in place.

"You what?" she asked in a furious whisper, her eyes wide.

"I locked the door," I said, enunciating each word and enjoying the flush rising up her neck and cheeks.

Speaking of her cheeks, she put both hands on them and shook her head. "I can't believe you." She took a gulp of air and called out, letting her hands fall as she did. "Be right there." Her eyes swung to me again, snapping. "You need to move," she ordered in a stern whisper.

"Right then." I reached up to pull her panties back in place before stepping back with a grin.

She shimmied her hips off the table and straightened her skirt. Walking to the door, she paused beside it, her body radiating tension from the back. After gulping breath, she opened the door.

A few minutes later, I walked outside into another drizzling afternoon. I was rock hard with need and pleased as punch. I could wait endlessly to bury my cock inside Olivia if I had more interludes like that.

Chapter Eight

OLIVIA

I closed the door to my office and leaned against it with a shaky sigh. It had been a mere hour since Liam had left, and I'd barely recovered. Every step I took, I could feel my thighs rub together and the damp silk between them. He'd brought me to the most explosive orgasm I'd ever had—right here, at work. Of all the stupid things I'd thought I could do, letting some internationally famous soccer star make me lose my mind during an examination was dead last on the list. My body was still reverberating from those heated moments, little shocks of pleasure pinging through me. Just thinking of it now made me wet again. If he walked into this room with me right now, I knew exactly what I wanted—him inside of me. Because he'd only given me a taste of what it could be like with him and it might damn me straight to hell, but I wanted more and I wanted it so badly, I could hardly stand it. My channel throbbed and a flush ran through my body.

I shoved away from the door and walked to my desk. By some miracle, I'd gotten through my next two appointments. I was relieved to finally have a few minutes to myself. I sank into the chair at my desk and clicked my computer on. Some dry, boring billing notes might get my mind off of Liam. I was a few minutes into typing up a report when my phone vibrated. I slipped it out of my pocket, glanced down at the screen and gasped.

Hello luv. What kind of complications would I need to have for another appointment with you?

I didn't recognize the number, but I knew without a doubt it was Liam. Who else would text me something like that? I had no idea how he'd gotten my personal number and certainly no idea what to do about it. I'd spent much of the afternoon torn between the depth of my desire for him and the need to regain control of my life. My God. I was putting my professional career on the line, all over a man. All I could think about was when I could see him again. I'd spent the last hour swinging between the poles of a raw, burning need I'd never experienced—ever—in my life, and berating myself for throwing my sanity and ethics out the window by giving into the madness he elicited inside. I couldn't let myself do this. It was insanity, pure and simple.

There is no need for an appointment with me. You're in good hands with the PT team.

Excellent. Let's have dinner.

My cheeks were hot and all I could think about was the feel of his fingers inside me. No dinner. We could not do dinner. I couldn't be around him because he made me completely insane.

No thank you.

I forced myself to immediately turn my phone off after that and turned back to writing up my reports for the week. The next few hours were the most inefficient use of time I'd ever experienced. I was like an engine that wouldn't turn over. I'd try to start writing and get about two or three sentences in and then look down at my phone, it's screen dark. The urge to turn it back on was beating like a drum, meanwhile I was still wet and could hardly think straight because of it. All these years I'd dismissed sex as a pointless endeavor unless you wanted to have kids. What couldn't have been more than ten minutes with Liam's lips and hands on me and my indifference to pleasure had been shattered spectacularly. He'd shaken me to the core.

I spun in my chair and looked out the windows over the skyline of Seattle. Lights sparkled in the night sky. I took a slow breath and finally gave up on pointlessly working. I'd go home and start fresh tomorrow. Surely by then, I'd get a grip on my body.

A short while later, I walked into my apartment. I lived a few blocks down the street from the clinic. It had never even crossed my mind to consider living further away. I was so work focused, I simply wanted the convenience. I kicked my shoes off by the door and hung up my dripping raincoat before walking into the kitchen and putting the kettle on for tea. My apartment was in an upper floor of a small building with rather quaint apartments. The kitchen wasn't much more than an alcove off the living room through a small archway. The entire apartment had hardwood floors and tall, arched windows, which let in ample light even on rainy days. That said, I was rarely home during the daytime, except on weekends.

I padded through the living room to my bedroom, quickly changing into a pair of soft fleece pants and a sweatshirt. It was early autumn in Seattle, which meant chilly weather. The radiators grumbled slightly when I turned up the heat on my way back into the kitchen. I heated leftovers in the microwave and settled on the couch with my laptop and my tea while I absently nibbled on my food. With the television rumbling in the background, I reviewed referrals. One of the luxuries of my job was the option to take or refuse cases. There were only a few exceptions to this. For example, Liam. Under no circumstances would the clinic turn down a high-profile case such as his.

Even though I experienced pangs of conscience over how much money we charged our patients, one thing I loved at the clinic was that the medical team would refer cases out to other specialists if they thought the injury in question required expertise we didn't have. We tended to focus more on joints, while there were a few other specialists nationally who were better suited for spinal injuries.

After a few chart reviews, I zapped off emails to the referral team regarding the cases in question. I tried to dig into some research we were doing on recovery times for different ACL repair procedures, but my mind kept wandering to Liam. With a sigh, I closed my laptop and started flipping through the channels, hoping to find something to nudge my mind out of its unsettled state. My cozy apartment with its comfy loveseat and ottoman and cheerful purple throw rugs felt lonely just now. It wasn't that I had no friends. Daisy was my dearest friend, and we had a small circle of friends that occasionally got together. My aunt was the only family I had to speak of, but we rarely saw each other. She lived in a small town roughly an hour outside of Seattle in the foothills of the Cascade Mountains. With my nearly relentless work schedule, I had precious time to drive out to visit her.

I couldn't pin down what it was, but something about Liam elicited this odd loneliness. I didn't like it. He made me want things I'd never wanted. For starters, another bone-melting orgasm would be just fine. It wasn't only that though. He was funny and sly and watching him with Alex let me know he was a good friend. As much as he projected a teasing, devil-may-care attitude, it was clear he had more depth to him than I'd guessed.

I stood up abruptly, restless with the disquiet I felt inside. I left the TV on because I didn't want to hear the echoing silence around me and walked into the bathroom to fill the tub. That's what I'd do. I loved baths. They were one of the few things that helped me unwind when I was tired and stressed. A few minutes later, I sank into the steaming hot water with a sigh. I rested my head against the tile wall and let the heat seep through me. Once I was warm all the way through, I grabbed the soap, quickly sliding it everywhere to wash the day away. When the bar of soap slid between my thighs in the course of cleaning, my mind and body flashed back to the feel of Liam's fingers working their magic. That was it. All it took was no more than a second, and I was hot all over and my channel throbbed.

Today had been eye opening in more ways than one. I'd meant it emphatically when I said sex was boring. Because it had been. Until Liam got a hold of me. We hadn't even technically had sex, but I knew beyond even the thought of a shadow of doubt that going further with him would be unlike anything I'd ever imagined. I nearly threw the soap into its dish and splashed water on my face. Nothing nudged my mind off the madness Liam elicited though, so I climbed out of the tub and ran my wrists under cold water, a quick trick to cool the body down. I supposed I did cool off, but when I was lying in bed, I could feel the pulse of my channel and the slick heat there.

I rolled up one last time and rested my head on my knees, my breath coming in steady heaves. I'd just finished a round of one hundred sit-ups.

"Well, your knee hasn't affected your stamina a bit," Tim Maxwell commented from beside me.

I lifted my head and snagged a towel on the mat. Wiping my face, I looked over at him. "Definitely not. Never thought I'd be bloody happy to grind through sit-ups, but it feels damn good to finally put some work into something."

Tim flashed a grin. He was my assigned physical therapist and was basically my shadow whenever I was in the gym. The clinic offered physical therapy on site and off. I opted for both because I wanted to make sure I didn't do something stupid when I was with the team for workouts, and I also wanted any chance I could get to encounter Olivia at the clinic. I leaned back on my hands and looked over at Tim. "Anyone ever mention you might as well be the model for that American doll? What the hell is it called?" I asked.

Tim flashed another grin, showing off his nearly perfect pearly whites. With his blonde hair, he was a dead ringer.

"You must mean the Ken doll. My boyfriend teases me about looking like that all the time. I keep telling him my eyes are brown, not blue."

I rolled onto my hip and pushed myself to standing. "I bet he bloody well does." I snagged a bottle of water and gulped some down before looking back to Tim who'd stood up with me. "What now?"

"Let's get you onto the treadmill," he said, gesturing for me to follow as he headed over a row of exercise machines.

We were at the clinic, so I wasn't as familiar with the equipment here. My gut coiled with slight anxiety. I was torn inside about how to feel as I'd gotten started with my physical therapy. On the one hand, I was in a blazing hurry to be fully recovered. On the other hand, I was dealing with an unfamiliar anxiety about not pushing my knee too far or too fast. I didn't want to blow my recovery by getting impatient. I hated the anxious feeling because anxiety wasn't something I experienced often, especially when it came to playing.

I ignored the feeling and followed Tim. He stopped by one of the machines and glanced back at me. "What's up?" he asked, his eyes scanning my face. "Are you in any pain?"

"Nah. I'm fine. I, ah... Well, are you sure my knee's ready to try running?" I finally asked.

Tim leaned his shoulder on the machine and nodded. "You could run right now, but we're only starting with some walking today. I'd like you to pick up your pace a little. This machine is almost a combo treadmill and elliptical. It's got a much lower swing than most ellipticals, but it takes the weight off your stride unlike a treadmill." He paused, his gaze considering. "I'd be nervous if I were you, but I promise I wouldn't suggest it if you weren't ready. You're a world-class athlete and you need this recovery to succeed. It will. Also, don't forget going too slow can hamper your recovery as well. We need your muscle memory to hold and prevent your muscles from trying to accommodate for the injury."

My logical brain knew every word Tim said made sense,

but it didn't erase my trepidation. I took a deep breath and nodded. I was beyond relieved that Tim and I got along. I'd liked him the first time I met him. He didn't hesitate to push me, but he was gracious and supportive. I'd been lucky so far in my years of playing and had yet to deal with physical therapy, but I'd heard about it from teammates. Ethan Walsh, another of my mates to be sent here from Britain, had suffered through a torn ACL last year and referred to his PT guy as his physical terrorist. I was bloody relieved to click with Tim and trust him. With that in mind, I followed his guidance and stepped onto the machine. He showed me how to adjust the speed and a few other settings and got me started.

A short while later, I walked out of the changing room, relieved to have easily gotten through the fast-paced walking Tim had me start. It felt so painless, I'd tried to persuade him I should step it up to an actual running speed. He'd firmly declined with a roll of his eyes. Another thing I liked about him was he had no problem standing up to me.

I paused in the area where the hallways intersected at the clinic. Olivia's office was down a hall to my left, while her usual examination room was down a different hall to the right. She'd been ignoring my texts, so I was driven to find her, so driven it should have rattled me. I kept telling myself it was about sex because that was the easy answer to my attraction to her. It wasn't that sex wasn't part of the equation, but more that there was a part of me drawn to her on such an elemental level, it struck me at my core. I glanced from left to right and back, contemplating my best option to see her. I settled on going to her office because there would be no one else to navigate there. If I went to the area where the examination rooms were, I'd have to check in with the receptionist, and I knew there might be questions because I didn't have an appointment. I also had no reason for an appointment. Knowing Olivia's tendency to be proper, I didn't want to give her more reason to push me away much as it went against my grain. I bloody loved getting under her skin like that. Not because I thought it was the least bit improper, but because I liked seeing her riled, and I oddly liked when she tried to hold onto her prim and proper side.

I reached the door to her office. The usual me would boldly open the door and step inside. I wasn't confident she'd be there, but I felt a thread of uncertainty inside. I wasn't used to wanting someone so much. It wasn't just the physical desire, but that I wanted to see her smile, to see the tight lines of her face soften and to hold her close. I shifted my shoulders and almost turned away, but the pull was too strong. I rapped quickly on the door and was surprised to hear her call for me to come in. Well, she didn't know it was me just yet. As I reached for the doorknob, my entire body tightened in anticipation and a curl of happiness rolled through me. I didn't know what it was about her, but it was pure joy to be around her.

I opened to door and stepped through, closing and locking it so quickly I hoped she wouldn't notice. Olivia hadn't even looked up. She was seated in a chair at her desk, leaning forward to read something on her screen. A few curls had fallen loose from the knot atop her head. I itched to walk over and untie that knot and run my hands through her silky curls. I took a few steps into the room, wondering when she'd notice me. I was at her desk by the time she did. She clicked something on her keyboard and spun in her chair to glance up. Her gorgeous green eyes widened and a flush rose on her cheeks.

"Liam. I, um..." She paused and bit her lip, which sent a jolt of lust straight to my groin. She gave her head a shake, which sent another curl unspooling to dangle along her cheek. "I didn't know you were stopping by," she finally said after a few beats.

She surprised me by standing up and coming around the desk. Crossing her arms, she leaned her hip against the desk and pinned her eyes on me, her expression going all serious and stern. I loved it.

"You haven't replied to my texts," I said by way of greeting.

Olivia's mouth tightened further, but her cheeks flushed a lovely cherry red. "Liam, we can't..." Her words trailed off and she looked straight at me. "You know I can't do this! You're my patient and you're a crazy famous soccer star. What do you want with me anyway? You can have your pick of women."

She stood maybe three feet away from me. I closed the distance in two strides and stopped just in front of her. Her scent drifted to me, a hint of honey and sweetness. My cock hardened. "As far as I'm concerned, I'm not your patient anymore. If I was, I'd have an appointment with you, and you know I don't." I paused to gauge her response and was satisfied to see her eyes narrow, but she didn't say a word. "As for the rest, that's nonsense. I'm just a man and I want you. Only you."

I heard my words and distantly wondered why I wasn't startled by them. I should've been. I was stumbling headlong into a madness of my own making here. I didn't want 'one' woman ever. I hewed to keeping relationships quite casual and appreciated the side perk of being a recognized sports star, which offered ample casual opportunities. Oh, there were plenty of women looking for more, but I avoided them like the plague. I wasn't the worst of my mates, certainly not. I minded my business and made sure every woman left my bed thoroughly satisfied.

But Olivia. She was something else altogether. I wanted her with a ferocity I didn't recognize, and I couldn't have turned away from it if I tried. She was quiet, her eyes pinned to me. I reached for her, curling my palms over her forearms and slowly unfolding them. I slid my hands down until I reached hers and held them in mine. My heart was pounding —a hard, fast beat against my ribs. I idly stroked a thumb over the soft skin of her wrist, feeling the flutter of her pulse underneath.

Her breath drew in sharply and her eyes stayed locked on mine. She was in her scrubs again today, a bright blue pair that contrasted with her dark hair and creamy complexion. She shifted on her feet. "Liam, this is crazy," she finally said with a soft sigh.

I shook my head and freed one of her hands to lift mine and give into the urge to untie her hair. With a flick, the curls tumbled loose around her shoulders. *Sweet hell.* With her hair down, she nearly took my breath away. Her curls were a dark, wild riot. They hinted at the passion she tried so hard to hide. I sifted my hand through them, savoring the feel of her silky locks sliding through my fingers. I stepped closer and slid my other hand down her spine, pulling her close against me. I could feel ripples running through her body, while mine was tight as a drum, my cock so hard I could hardly bear it. But bear it I would. Because the challenge Olivia offered only grew more tempting.

I wasn't accustomed to having to do anything on someone else's terms, but as much as I wanted to rush this, I knew I couldn't. Olivia would knock me back, no matter how tempted she was. So, I wouldn't rush, but I wasn't leaving her office without at least another taste of her lips.

I slowly leaned back, just far enough to loosen my hand from her curls and remove her glasses, setting them on the desk beside us. The air around us was heavy, laden with the pulsing beat of desire. I wanted to think I was in control, but the truth was, it was just barely. I felt as if I was freefalling. Pausing to look down at her, I threaded my hand into her hair again and dipped my head. Even though it took every ounce of discipline I had, I moved slowly. I could hardly have stood it if she didn't let me kiss her, but for some reason I had to know she wanted it enough not to push me away.

Olivia's eyes darkened to a deep green, and her breath

came in shallow gasps. She startled me when she slipped her hand up around my neck and yanked me to her, pausing when my lips were but a whisper away from hers. "Dammit, don't make me any crazier than I already am," she whispered fiercely. The feel of her lips brushing mine when she spoke snapped my control.

Chapter Ten

OLIVIA

By the time Liam fit his mouth over mine and finally—finally!—kissed me, I was about out of my mind. In the weeks since our last kiss, I'd almost convinced myself I'd exaggerated how good it felt to kiss him. I was wrong, so very, very wrong. The moment I looked up and saw him standing in my office, heat roared through me. I tried to hold onto my sanity, but I couldn't. When he was near, I was torn inside. There was the rational part of my brain that knew what I was doing was wrong, so very wrong. Yet, the raw need I felt for him overpowered everything else, most certainly my reason. With his hand cupping my bottom and holding me firm against him, I gasped when he arched his hips into mine, the hard ridge of his cock brushing against my clit. I almost came right then and there—that's how tightly wound I was.

If someone had asked me how I liked to be kissed, I'd have shrugged and said it didn't matter. Kisses were just as boring as sex, or so I thought until Liam kissed me. Now I knew I liked the bone-melting combination of slow, long, hot and deep—his tongue alternated between deep sweeps inside, tangling with mine, and then slow traces around my mouth, nips on my bottom lips and overpowering kisses in between. By the time he tore his lips free for air, I was gasping and nearly frantic inside. He looked down at me, his eyes a blur of blue, his gaze so intent it sent my belly in a slow flip. I was drenched and shifted my legs restlessly, seeking relief from the pressure building inside. His cock was hot and hard against me, and I wanted him inside me. Now.

His eyes searched my face before he turned, angling us so my hips bumped against the desk. He curled his hands around my hips and lifted me, swiftly stepping in between my knees and pulling me flush against him. I was so sensitive, I moaned at the subtle pressure of his cock against my clit. I'd gone mad, plain and simple. I forgot where we were and forgot all the reasons why I shouldn't be doing this. I curled my legs around his hips and arched into him.

Shoving his shirt up, I sighed at the feel of his skin under my hands—hot and smooth, his hard muscles flexing under my touch. He brushed my curls out of the way and trailed kisses down my neck, sending hot shivers through me. Meanwhile, he cupped my breasts in his hands, brushing his thumbs back and forth over my nipples, which were tight and achy. Sensation teemed inside as he shoved my top up. He lifted his head, his mouth curling at one corner. "You're naughtier than you let on," he murmured.

By some miracle, I formed a partial thought, wondering what he was talking about. My question must have shown on my face. "This is hardly a bra," he said, snapping the slender strap and running his fingers lightly over the sheer silk.

My cheeks heated, and need scored me straight to my core. I forgot to respond when he dipped his head and swirled his tongue over a nipple. I cried out when his lips closed over it, drenching the silk. He pulled away with a little nip of his teeth and turned his attention to the other nipple. I did like things to be in balance. By the time he lifted his head again, I was grinding my hips against him. I'd never have believed I could come just from the feel of his mouth on my nipples, but I almost did.

I wanted more. I tore at his jeans, but he stepped back and stopped me, his grip on my wrists firm. His expression was pained as he looked back at me. "Liam, I need…"

He shook his head. "Not this. Not now," he said in a low voice.

My need was coiled so tight, it lashed impatiently within. "That's not fair," I said, almost churlishly. Since I'd lost my hold on reason and blown past boundaries I held dear, it annoyed me he was putting the brakes on. There was that and the pounding need seeking release.

He eased his grip and stroked a hand down my belly, past the waistband of my scrubs. His palm cupped me through the silk of my panties. My channel throbbed, slick with wet heat. His eyes caught mine. "I want to bury myself so deep inside you we both forget where we end and begin. I don't want to rush, so it won't be here."

I stared into his deep blue gaze, his words slamming into me. A distant warning bell rang in my mind, but it was faint, drowned out in the storm of emotion and desire nearly tearing me apart inside. He was so confident, so positive there would be more, that I should've been angered and sought to snatch control back. But I was well and truly lost in this moment and latched onto the promise in his words, nearly frantic to demand we leave right now and go somewhere else if that's the only way I'd feel him buried inside me.

As he spoke, he began to drag a finger back and forth over the silk wet silk. My hips arched into his touch. In the midst of the heavy quiet with nothing but the sound of our breath, my desk phone rang. I jumped and started to scramble back on the desk.

"Oh no," he said, his gruff, haughty tone sending a ripple through me.

He shoved my panties out of the way and slid two fingers inside me just as he circled his thumb over my swollen clit. I came so hard and fast, I saw stars.

Liam slowly pulled his hand away, neatly put the silk between my thighs and tugged my pants back up to my waist. I was so stunned, I could barely think, much less move. Before I realized it, he'd straightened my shirt, pulling it down over my wet bra. My body was reverberating as awareness filtered back in. My phone beeped, indicating whoever had called had left a message.

I couldn't seem to snap out of it. I wanted to curl up in Liam's arms and forget about everything else right now. He reached up and brushed my hair back, sifting his fingers through the messy curls. "What do I have to do to get you to have dinner with me?" he asked softly.

I swallowed against the wave of emotion inside. I didn't know what this madness was, but I didn't have it in me to fight against it. Not now. Not when I didn't think I could take it if I didn't get more than this with him. "I'll have dinner with you," I whispered, feeling my cheeks heat.

He smiled, almost boyishly. He let his hands fall and stepped away. I instantly missed the heat of him, the pure strength of his nearness. "Tomorrow night then?" he asked, his eyes locked to mine.

"Okay. Um, where?"

I felt silly and unmoored. With pleasure echoing in my body, I couldn't think too clearly. I'd so removed myself from the world of dating that I wasn't familiar with the basics.

Liam saved me and gave a firm nod. "I'll text you, but you'd better respond. If you don't, I'll come find you. You know what happens when I do that," he said with a sly grin.

I blushed so hotly, I was surprised I didn't burst into flames. He straightened his jeans and stepped to my desk again, helping me off. I wondered if I was having something like the opposite of an out of body experience, an in-body experience if there was such as thing. I was hyperaware of every move he made, my body attuned to him. The air around us felt weighted. I glanced up to find his eyes on me. He dipped his head and dropped a rather chaste kiss on my cheek.

"Until tomorrow then."

At that, he turned and left my office. I watched as he walked away, my medical eye tracking his stride and pleased to see he had only the slightest hitch in his gait. When the door closed behind him, I turned and walked to the windows, staring out over the skyline. Puget Sound was visible in the distance, boats dotting the water. After a few moments, my pulse was close to normal. I ran my hands through my hair and wound it back into a knot, snagging the elastic that had fallen to the floor earlier when Liam set my curls loose. I put my glasses on and calmly sat down at my desk. I managed to check my voice mail, beyond relieved it was nothing more than a message from one of the other doctors at the clinic about an upcoming meeting.

Later that evening, I pushed through the door to the Desert Isle Café and glanced around for Daisy. I'd been back and forth all afternoon about whether to talk to Daisy about Liam, but when I saw our friend Harper with her, that made my mind up. It wasn't that I wouldn't look to Harper for advice, but more I wasn't ready to bare my soul to more than one person at a time. For the first time in my life, I felt completely out of my element. I'd been so confident I'd never go gaga over a guy. And here I was gaga over Liam, so far gone I'd made out with him—big time—twice at work.

I considered myself intelligent, and I knew I was when it came to academics and medicine. My record of straight A's ran all the way back to kindergarten. Socially, well, that's where I floundered. I hadn't ever had to worry about my anxiety about dating and men because it hadn't interested me. Looking back, I could see I simply hadn't stumbled across anyone who I had genuine chemistry with. I almost laughed aloud. I was so out of my element here. Considering what lay between Liam and

I, describing it as chemistry was almost silly—more like a wild, burning conflagration. Being a surgeon had given me too much faith in the clinical lens of considering the human body. With Liam, I'd quickly discovered I'd been foolishly confident in my ability to stay detached. The physical drive to connect with him was a powerful enough force, I was utterly failing at holding back the tide. There was that and the underlying pull I felt—a pull that went beyond pure desire and didn't fit into the tidy classifications my medical mind found comfort in.

I waved when I saw Daisy glance to the door. After grabbing a coffee at the counter, I threaded my way to the table where they were and sat down with a sigh. "Hey there," I said as I slipped my arms out of my damp raincoat and hung it over the back of my chair.

Harper Jacobs grinned at me. "Hey you! Hope you don't mind I crashed your weekly coffee date with Daisy."

"Of course not," I said before taking a long sip of my coffee. "You're always invited."

Harper nodded and leaned back in her chair. "I know, but I'm hardly ever on this side of town." With her glossy straight brown hair, warm blue eyes and athletic build, Harper evoked a sense of down-to-earth outdoorsy-ness. She'd moved to the small town outside of Seattle where Daisy and I grew up during middle school and quickly become a friend. While Daisy and I were both academically oriented, Harper was the friend who dragged us out of the house. She'd been a track star in college, but her potential for more had skidded sideways after she'd been raped by an acquaintance. He'd been on the track team for a nearby university. Daisy and I had been there when her world blew apart. It had only been the last year or so that she'd finally seemed back to herself. She swore she'd never date again. She'd gotten her degree in physical therapy and consulted on cases for several clinics in Seattle. She and I made referrals to each other occasionally.

I leaned over and gave her shoulders a squeeze. "It's nice you're here today. How've you been?"

Harper shrugged. "You know, busy with work. I'm guessing the same for you?'

I nodded, but the moment I did, I thought of Liam's fingers buried inside me when I came just a few hours ago. I swatted the thought away.

"Of course Olivia's busy," Daisy added. "She's a workaholic."

I glared at her. "No different than you."

Daisy grinned. "Maybe not. How's your latest sports star doing?"

I felt my cheeks heating and ignored it. I felt tossed and turned by Liam. I was putting way too much on the line, and I had no idea how to stop the madness. Before I had a chance to reply, Harper spoke.

"You mean Liam Reed?" she asked. "The clinic across town is all bitchy the Seattle Stars didn't contract with them to see their players. It's all so silly. I told the office manager there to remember the insurance pays the same. I decided not to point out you're a better surgeon than anyone they have on staff," Harper said with a sly grin.

Daisy winked. "I bet you never thought you'd get all the hot guys just because you're the best surgeon around."

"Oh my God," I said with a roll of my eyes.

Daisy looked to Harper. "When we were here the other week, Liam stopped by with Alex Gordon, the hot goalie for the Stars. They were quite nice with those sexy British accents, and Liam wants to make a move on Olivia," Daisy said with a wink as she leaned back in her chair.

I gave up fighting my blush and looked to Harper. "She's being ridiculous."

"No I'm not! You said he wanted to make a move on you, and trust me, he does. That man all but ate you up with his eyes." Daisy looked to Harper. "Olivia's being all proper and says he's her patient. The surgery's over, so I think she should go for it."

It was nearly killing me to hold it in that I'd already had the two most explosive orgasms of my life with Liam, but I couldn't say anything. Not here. Harper rolled her eyes at Daisy before turning to me. "Nice to hear the guy half the world is drooling over noticed you. You're amazing and you never give anyone a chance." She glanced back to Daisy, her eyes narrowing. "He might not technically be her patient now, but if Olivia wants to set some boundaries, don't give her grief about it."

I took a gulp of coffee, nearly bursting out in laughter at what had happened to my boundaries. After another gulp of coffee, I managed to look at Harper. "Thank you for a dose of reason. How about we talk about something else?"

Daisy giggled, but Harper gamely shifted gears, asking me for feedback on a knee surgery that had gone awry for one of her clients. It had only been in the last year that we'd even joked about dating and men around Harper. Aside from the fact I didn't want to dwell on Liam right now, I was so relieved to see her relaxed and easy-going about the topic I didn't want to unintentionally carry things too far.

Hours later that night, I lay in bed with thoughts of Liam running laps in my brain. This was *so* not me. I usually got stuck on medical topics and often found myself up late at night looking at data from recovery rates and reviewing surgery videos. I didn't lie in bed longing for anyone. I was restless and needy. I'd liked to have thought yet another orgasm under his magic touch would have slaked my need, but it only seemed to make it worse. The thing was, it wasn't plain physical release I needed. I needed Liam.

Chapter Eleven

LIAM

I leaned back on my hands on the bench and watched my team practice. As boring as it was, relatively speaking, I had learned a thing or two. I was bloody impatient to be back in play, but I was starting to recognize I could get through this time without losing my mind. They were practicing inside today, as it was drizzling yet again. It was cool enough now the coaching staff deemed it not good for our muscles to practice outside when the weather was like this. After a final play, I watched my teammates file slowly toward the locker room.

Coach strolled to the bench and sat down beside me, resting his elbows on his knees and looking ahead. "How's the knee feeling?" he asked.

I stretched my leg out and flexed it again, sensing only a slight hitch and very little soreness. ""Good. I think. Tim says I'm moving right along."

Coach looked to the side, catching my eyes. "So I hear. Dr. Monroe spoke with him this morning. If all stays on track, it sounds like you'll be back in action in under two months from now." He paused as if considering his words.

"You know, I wasn't so sure you'd show up like I asked. I hope you understand why I did."

I nodded. "Right. Can't say I was happy about it at first. The team is what matters. I'm new enough here that if I dropped out of sight, it wouldn't be good for the rest of the team. Plus, I've actually learned a few things," I said with a grin. "On the pitch, I have a sense of who's where, but you only know what's within a certain range. This many hours of watching practice and tapes gives me a better sense of how everyone functions once the play's in motion."

Coach smiled, just barely. He stood and held his hand out, giving me a tug as I stood and walked alongside him. A few minutes later, I met Alex just outside the locker room, and we headed out together. Tugging my hood up, I tucked my hands in my pockets as we walked through the drizzle to Desert Isle Café nearby, the very place we'd encountered Olivia a few weeks ago. The second she flashed through my thoughts, a jolt of heat hit me. I'd hardly stopped thinking about her if I was honest.

Alex, being the best mate he was, held the door and gestured me through in front of him. I joked about it, but despite the fact he looked like a beast, he was the most gentlemanly of us all. He was tall and solid as a rock. I didn't think I was being biased when I said he was the best goalkeeper in the world because most everyone who knew anything about football agreed with me.

Stepping out of the chilly rain was a relief. I tossed my hood back and walked to the counter, my eyes scanning the crowded café, hoping to see Olivia. Alex nudged my shoulder. I turned and realized the line had moved ahead while I was standing there like fool looking for a woman. Of course, only I knew that, but still.

"Your Dr. Bowen isn't here, mate," Alex said.

I glanced to him and rolled my eyes. "Wasn't..." I started to deny I'd been looking for her and then decided I didn't give a damn. "Fine, maybe I was looking for her. She's nice."

And so damn hot you got off thinking about her in the shower this morning. I kept that little detail to myself and continued. "Plus, you're the one who thought she was so great because she was focused on me and not the team."

Alex chuckled softly and looked away to order a coffee when the person in front of us stepped away from the counter. After we both ordered, we stood aside to wait. Alex leaned against the counter just as two women approached us. Per usual, Alex barely acknowledged them, nodding his head slightly. Under usual circumstances, I'd be the one to engage in easy banter, yet I wasn't the slightest bit interested and, in fact, felt impatient with the whole thing.

Somehow I managed to say hello. I stood there awkwardly while one of the women, quite beautiful with long, silky blonde hair, a willowy figure and blue eyes, stood a bit too close for my comfort.

"Is it just me, or do you happen to look exactly like Liam Reed?" she said with a slow smile.

I felt Alex's shoulders shake slightly, although unless you knew him like I did you wouldn't notice he was amused.

"Not just you. Liam and I are one and the same," I deadpanned. "If you don't mind, I'm rather busy right now."

The woman looked back and forth between Alex and I, a smile teasing at the corners of her mouth. "Well then, if you find you're not so busy later..." Her words trailed off as she scribbled a number on a scrap of paper she dragged out of her purse. She brazenly slipped it into my pocket and sauntered off. I had to give it to her for clearly being a master. She had enough sense to back off at my cool response, but made it quite clear she was available. Even a few weeks ago, I'd have been thinking about when I'd be calling her. Instead, I was indifferent beyond objectively appreciating her boldness.

Alex angled to face me and shook his head slowly. "You've got it bad," he said.

"For her?" I asked, sidestepping because I knew he was referring to Olivia. He knew me too well.

He rolled his eyes. "No. Dr. Bowen," he said flatly with a knowing smile.

"I don't see Dr. Bowen anywhere here," I countered, enjoying calling Olivia 'doctor.'

"Exactly. I usually rely on you to flirt enough to keep me out of the fray. Ever since you laid eyes on Dr. Bowen, you haven't noticed anyone else."

I wanted to tell Alex he was way off base, but he wasn't and he'd hadn't known me as long as he had for nothing. I shrugged. "So what? Even you have to admit she's gorgeous."

"I'd have to be blind not to notice that, mate. Do me a favor, don't toy with her. She's nice. I don't think she's much for casual."

This wasn't the first time Alex had warned me away from a woman. He wasn't one to judge, but he had a protective streak that extended to the whole wide world. I shifted my shoulders, slightly uncomfortable. The depth of need I felt for Olivia went so far beyond my usual interest in women, I had an inkling there was much more than a little fun at play. Yet, it wasn't something I wanted to ponder. I was relieved to have our names called at that moment. Alex stepped past me quickly and snagged both of our coffees.

We walked the remaining block back to our flat on a side street. I hoped Alex didn't plan to mention Olivia again. Not when all I could think about was seeing her tonight. I didn't want to worry about what any of it meant.

"If you're looking for more than casual, Dr. Bowen just might be the woman for you," Alex said off hand as he toed his shoes off by the door and hung his jacket on the hooks by the door.

His comment sent my heart to drumming. Only Alex would pick up on the depth of my attraction to Olivia. I wanted to ask him why he said that and what he thought. Along with all kinds of questions I'd never even considering contemplating about any woman. I looked to him and couldn't bring myself to push back with sarcasm, my usual refuge. I stared blankly at him, while the feeling in my chest tightened and I inexplicably thought about my mum and the look on my dad's face a few days after her funeral.

With a mental shake, I turned away and hung up my coat, escaping to the bathroom for a shower that I didn't really need. After my shower, I texted Olivia. I wouldn't tell her that I'd spent hours wondering where she might want to go to dinner because I'd felt bloody ridiculous about it. I'd discovered Seattle was awash in allegedly amazing restaurants. I wasn't much for fancy, so I'd finally settled on a place recommended by one of the stadium staff.

Hello luv. Picking you up at 6. Tell me where to find you.

I set my phone down and strolled to the window in my bedroom. The rain was still falling and blurred the skyline, drops rolling down the glass. I gripped the ends of the towel tossed over my shoulders and took a slow breath, testing the flexion of my knee. The anxiety that rumbled under the surface whenever I thought about my knee was gradually starting to abate now that my recovery seemed to be going smoothly. My restlessness over not playing likely wasn't going anywhere until I was cleared to play again, but it felt more manageable.

My phone buzzed on the dresser and I turned to snag it. I'd never impatiently waited for a woman's text in my life, but when it came to Olivia, all bets were off. Her reply made me smile.

Not necessary for you to pick me up. I can meet you there.

I could see the furrow between her brows and feel the thread of proper in her tone. She still wasn't so sure what to do about me. Little did she know I wasn't so sure what to do about her. Yet, I'd be damned if I'd let that hold me back.

Yes, luv. I'm picking you up. No arguing allowed.

I didn't put the phone down this time, watching while

the dotted line appeared in my screen, letting me know she was replying.

Are you really going to be bossy?

Oh. This was perfect. I hadn't realized I might be pushing her to push back, but I loved that she did. Lust lashed lightly inside, and my cock hardened. I couldn't help but run my hand over the towel. I tapped out my reply with one hand while I stroked my cock with the other. I didn't dare give in any more though because it would be sadly unsatisfying.

Bossy works for me. You can boss me too. I'd quite like that.

Holy hell, I was so bloody hard for her, I needed to stop this madness. All we were doing was texting.

Fine then. My address is 124 Castle Street.

Leave it to her to be direct and matter-of-fact. Her quick reply almost disappointed me. Sparring with her turned me on like crazy. I pushed back again, needling her because I couldn't help myself.

Fine then. Wear your hair down.

I set the phone down and nearly groaned at the need clawing me. Olivia was going to kill me. How was it possible to want someone so much that all it took was a small banter of texting and I was on the verge of taking matters into my own hands just to ease the lust whipping inside?

My phone buzzed on the dresser.

No.

I picked up my phone again.

Please.

Chapter Twelve

OLIVIA

I paced by the arched window in my apartment, my arms crossed over my chest and a restless anxiety pushing me in a tight rotation in front of the window. What had I been thinking, agreeing to let Liam pick me up? It felt like we'd already crossed too many boundaries and him seeing where I lived was yet another. His text had been straightforward enough, but it was as if I could feel him through the words he typed—his sly, boyish grin, his tendency to push me just enough to get my back up. When he'd told me to wear my hair down, I got annoyed and said no. Then, he said please and it totally turned me on. Me, the woman who found sex dry and boring, was turned on by a cocky soccer player using the word 'please.' I knew he had his pick of women because most sports stars did. In fact, it had surprised me slightly when some model perfect girlfriend hadn't shown up the day of the surgery to wait in the waiting room. We were accustomed to that at the clinic.

I'd once had to listen to one woman sob and carefully try not to smear her mascara when I had to give the bad news to her football star boyfriend that he'd torn his ACL one too many times and likely wouldn't play professionally again. It seemed as if all thoughts led back to Liam. I instantly skipped tracks to considering how American football was so rough on athletes. Liam called himself a footballer, as did the rest of the entire world. Yet, that football, or rather soccer as commonly denoted in the US, came with some risk, but it wasn't so brutal. Liam's meniscus tear would become a distant memory for him. His worry was most likely about how it might affect his speed and agility in play.

My thoughts jumped back to worrying about the complete insanity of what I was doing. I shouldn't be doing anything with Liam, most certainly not having dinner with him. Only about a hundred times today, I'd considered texting him to cancel. Yet, I never did, and he'd be here any minute. I circled back in my tiny loop of pacing, almost jumping at the sound of the knock on the door. My heart was beating wildly, and I was hot and cold at once. I ran a hand over my curls. I'd left my hair down. I'd never bothered to reply to his plea, but I couldn't have said no again. Me, who never worried about what I wore, had obsessed over what to wear tonight and finally settled on long cotton skirt that hugged my hips and flared around my ankles. Daisy had given it to me for my birthday last year. It was a deep shade of green and, according to her, brought out my eyes. It could pass off as a casual skirt and be nice at the same time. I'd paired it with a white blouse that cinched at the neck and fit loosely. Knowing it was raining out, I'd opted for a practical pair of ankle high leather boots.

I walked to the door and stopped in front of it. I was ridiculously nervous. I tried to remember the last date I'd been on, and I thought it was in college with a guy Daisy had tried to pair me up with. He'd been nice enough and handsome enough, but I was pretty sure I bored him silly and the sex sure had bored me silly. I certainly hadn't worried about what to wear.

On the heels of a deep breath, I opened the door. Liam

stood there, filling the space with his broad muscled shoulders. His dark hair gleamed under the lights in the hall, and his blue eyes were bright and locked onto me.

"Hello luv," he said.

I'd have to get used to his voice. Every time he spoke, his British accent sent a little curl through my belly. Pushing back against how pleased I was to see him, I arched a brow. "Must you call me that?" I couldn't admit I was annoyed with myself for secretly enjoying that he called me that, so I projected it onto him.

One side of his mouth hooked in a slow smile. "Yes. I must," he said with a firm nod. "Shall we go?"

I was nodding before I thought and started to step into the hallway.

"Do you need a jacket?" he asked, a second before I almost locked myself out of my apartment. That's how flighty Liam made me. I forgot my coat, forgot my purse, and even my keys and was about to traipse off with him.

"Oh right!" I spun around, my eyes scanning for my raincoat. I spied it flung on a chair in the kitchen. I scurried over to snag it, calling over my shoulder as I did. "You can come in. I have to find my purse," I said.

I pulled my jacket on and saw him step inside and lean his shoulder against the wall by the door. His eyes traveled around the apartment, and I wondered what he thought. I imagined he lived in much nicer digs. It wasn't that I didn't have a nice apartment, but it was small and simple. I could afford more, but I didn't think it was worth the bother since I worked so much. The loveseat, an ottoman and a large chair took up most of the living room. A fireplace I rarely used sat dark. The kitchen was a small nook with a round table and chairs. I had enough taste to care about my space, so I had brightly colored rugs and sheer white curtains, along with artwork on the walls.

I didn't see my purse anywhere and wondered where it was. Even a search in my bedroom didn't turn it up. As a last resort, I checked the bathroom and found it there on the sink counter, precisely where I'd wandered when I was texting Liam and needed to clean my glasses. I grabbed it and returned to the living room.

"Okay, I found everything."

"Everything?" Liam asked, the dark slash of a brow arcing up.

"Well, maybe not everything, but all I need for now."

He nodded and pushed his shoulder off the wall, holding the door as I walked through.

I'd wondered where he planned to take me and even wondered if he was driving. I quickly learned he wasn't driving when he led me to the light rail system. Despite the soft rain falling, the railcar was crowded. Liam startled me when he curled his hand around mine and pulled me close to his side as the bustle of people jostled me. I glanced around the railcar at one point and noticed several women unabashedly eyeing him. Whether they knew who he was, he was a magnet simply because he was mouth-wateringly hand-some. It felt strange to be with him like this. No matter my reservations about our quite recent doctor-patient relation-ship, I wasn't used to going anywhere with a man, much less a man who was pursuing me the way Liam was. I wasn't accustomed to the kind of attention he gave me—as we rode along, his eyes flicked down, and it felt as if he was touching me everywhere he looked. My nipples tightened, and I shifted my legs, feeling that restless need unfurl inside.

We got off by the airport with me still wondering where Liam was taking me. He paused on the sidewalk, his eyes scanning the row of businesses and then turned to the right. I could sense he was measuring his stride and resisted the urge to tell him he was clearly recovering nearly perfectly. He had the slightest hitch in his gait and nothing more. I didn't really want to go all doctor on him, so I held my tongue as we walked quietly through the softly falling rain. Somewhere along the way, his palm found its way to my low back, a warm point of contact that I savored.

He paused and looked to his side. "Here we are," he announced.

I couldn't help but smile. I hadn't been paying attention to precisely where we were because I'd been too distracted by the heat of Liam's palm on my back. We stood in front of one of my absolute favorite restaurants—13 Coins. By some sleight of hand, 13 Coins was all things at once. Years ago, it had started as a diner and morphed into something else with a massive menu that offered everything from diner basics to high-end gourmet meals. It was a place where you could feel comfortable wearing just about anything. I loved it because the food was amazing, the atmosphere comfortable, and it happened to have been my parents' favorite restaurant. When I was little, they used to load me up in the car and drive the hour plus to get here for Sunday brunch once a month. It was also where they'd gone every year for their anniversary.

I looked from the entrance to him. A slow smile stretched across his face. "Have I decided on a good place, then?"

"One of my favorites. Have you been here before?"

A smile stretched across his face. He was clearly pleased with himself. With subtle pressure, he nudged me through the entrance and out of the rain. "Eh, no. One of the guys at the stadium told me about it."

I flipped my hood back and gave my jacket a gentle shake. Liam's palm had left my back while he ran a hand over his damp hair. He'd eschewed the use of his hood, leaving his hair damp from the heavy drizzle. I missed his touch already. The entryway had a few people waiting, but it wasn't too bad for a Saturday evening. Liam stepped to the reception desk and before he even spoke, the woman working there smiled the moment she saw him. "Mr. Reed, you're right on time," she said with a glance to her watch. She picked up two menus and gestured for him to follow. "Right this way."

In moments, we were seated at one of the booths. 13 Coins had tall, leather backed seats that stretched to the ceiling, creating a warm, cozy feeling no matter which booth you were seated in. The space was all gleaming mahogany wood with leather. Though it was always busy, and I do mean always, the noise was never too much with the private booths. As with most older diners, the restaurant was open 24 hours a day with a menu so extensive one could eat there for every meal every day of the week and barely make a dent in the choices.

The hostess hardly granted me a glance, her eyes flicking to Liam even when she was taking my drink order. Needing something to take the edge off the wild restlessness inside, I ordered a pomegranate martini. Liam ordered a dark beer. The hostess went her way, and Liam leaned back with a sigh, his deep blue eyes bright in the soft lighting. "So tell me why this place is so amazing."

I fiddled with the place setting, unrolling the crisp white napkin around it and laying it on my lap as I replied. "It's been around forever. Well, maybe not forever but over fifty years. Trust me when I say it's a favorite of many, not just me. You can have everything from biscuits and gravy to glazed fresh caught salmon."

He cocked his head to the side. "Biscuits with gravy? A bit odd if you ask me."

"Oh, they're delicious. Must be an American thing."

"Odd, I say. Do you select what kind of biscuit? Say chocolate, or other?"

"Chocolate biscuits? Now that's odd."

Our waiter arrived to hear the tail end of our back and forth. He glanced between us. "Language barrier," he announced with a grin.

Liam and I swung to him simultaneously. The waiter's grin widened. "Brits call cookies biscuits. A chocolate cookie would be horrible with gravy. I'm sure you'd both agree," he said, his eyes bouncing between us as he served our drinks. He wore the usual black slacks and crisp white shirt for the staff there. "I'm Forrest by the way, and I'll be your server tonight. Would you like to hear our specials tonight?"

At Liam's nod, Forrest reeled off a list of specials. Liam graciously asked what Forrest would recommend from the menu when he started to flip through it. Forrest gamely began making a wide variety of suggestions. Liam's brows rose slightly with each additional dish. By the time Forrest finished, Liam had leaned back and started shaking his head. "That's a smashing long list. Can't remember a bit. Think I'll go with the cookies and gravy," he said with a slow grin and a wink in my direction.

I flushed and rolled me eyes. "How was I to know biscuits are cookies to you? It's not like you knew what I meant either. Anyway, are you sure you want that for dinner? It's kind of a breakfast thing."

Liam nodded firmly. "I love gravy, and I love breakfast."

I glanced to Forrest. "If we're going to eat breakfast dishes, I'll go with an omelet."

"It's a breakfast dinner then," Forrest said with a grin. "Any appetizers to go with that?"

After we shook our heads, Forrest departed and I took a sip of my martini, savoring the sweet tang of pomegranate. Liam took a long drag on his beer and idly rolled the bottle around after he set it down, his eyes pinned to me. I wasn't accustomed to the kind of attention he gave me. I crossed and uncrossed my legs and took another few sips of my martini. It was safe to say Liam's mere presence was over- whelming for me. My comfort zone was at work where I called the shots and focused on dry, clinical details. Being with Liam elicited a constant sense of being off balance between my body's haywire response to him and my own warring emotions. I wished I had the suave social banter skills the hostess had. She'd seamlessly flirted with Liam.

Meanwhile, my brain went right to wondering what to say and how to say it.

Liam saved me from obsessing much longer. "So you must come here often if it's one of your favorites."

I shrugged. "As often as I get out, I suppose I come here a lot. Not as much as when I was little. My parents used to bring me here every month for Sunday brunch. We lived about an hour outside of Seattle, and it was an event."

Something flickered in his eyes, but I didn't know what it was. "Do they still live nearby?" he asked, the next logical question.

"Not for a long time. They died in a car accident when I was ten. There's no need to apologize," I said, warning him off. I'd given this answer so many times, I was used to people feeling they must say they were sorry. "My mother's twin sister raised me after that, and she's still right where I grew up."

His eyes had gone dark, and he was quiet for a long moment. "Perhaps it's not necessary, but I am sorry. It's hard to lose a parent, much less both at once the way you did."

Something about the look on his face evoked a strong sense of loss and pain. I didn't know why, but I knew it wasn't simply because he'd learned my parents had died. "Are you okay?" I asked, not knowing why I felt compelled to ask.

His jaw tightened, and he took a quick gulp of his beer before replying. "My mum died of a stroke. Just a few months ago," he said, his voice almost wondering as if he couldn't quite believe it had happened.

"Oh Liam, I'm so sorry," I said. Before I realized what I was doing, I reached across the table with one hand and curled it around his, giving a squeeze.

His shoulders tensed and then relaxed when he returned the squeeze. "Can't say I'm quite used to it yet."

"Is your family close?"

He nodded, his throat moving with a swallow. "I worry about my dad. I might've fought against coming to the team here, but I've two brothers and they're nearby in London. They all insisted I do just as I would've if mum was alive. I'm bloody relieved Alex signed with me. We've been best mates since we were but lads, and he knows how close I was to my mum. It's not as bad as it was, but then I suppose you know that."

My heart clenched at the sadness held in Liam's usually teasing gaze. It was plain as day he'd loved his mother and was still reverberating from her death. I wanted to smooth the edges of his pain and I hardly knew him. Not really. "I have an idea. Loss is a strange thing. I was so much younger than you are, so I'm guessing it was different. You never stop missing people you lose, but you do get used to it. It's almost like it sharpens all the good, and you learn memories can help eventually."

He was quiet, his eyes considering. He finally nodded slowly. At that moment, Forrest stopped by the table. I hadn't realized I'd nearly emptied my martini. "Another drink while you wait for your meal?"

Liam slipped his hand free of mine as he lifted his beer bottle, as if testing its weight. At his nod with mine following, Forrest spun away. Liam caught my eyes. "Thank you," he said gruffly. "Not everyone understands, but I can tell you do." He leaned back and gave his head a little shake. "This is the part where we awkwardly move on."

I grinned. I couldn't help it. We could be maudlin all evening if we dwelled on the topic, so I was happy to move on. Before I had a chance to say anything else, Forrest returned with our drinks. "Food will be ready in just a few," he said as he kept moving.

A while later, I was laughing so hard, I'd almost spit my food out. Aside from being so handsome and sexy he nearly melted me, Liam was a funny and engaging dinner companion. He'd declared the biscuits and gravy his new favorite dish and had been regaling me with stories about pranks he and Alex played on friends during grammar school, which I'd learned was the British equivalent of grade school.

After Liam paid for dinner, which I'd started to argue about and he'd pinned me with a glare, we walked out into the chilly drizzle. The street glittered under the lights cast onto its wet surface in the dark. Liam's palm was warm on my back as he guided me onto the railcar. We managed to find seats now that the work rush was over. Once we were seated, I became hyperaware of Liam's closeness. His thigh, every hard, muscled inch of it, rested against mine. My pulse skittered and heat coiled low in my belly. I couldn't help but glance up to find him looking down as if he'd been waiting. Without a word, he slid his hand onto my thigh, the heat of his touch branding me.

I tore my eyes away where they landed on an ad mounted directly across from us inside the rail car. It just so happened to be an ad for the Seattle Stars, Liam's new team. The ad featured a shot of Liam himself, his leg angled out as it connected with the ball. Even in a still photo, he conveyed a sense of power and motion. My pulse notched higher and my attention zeroed in on where his palm rested on my thigh. Desire, the very desire only Liam could elicit, rolled through me in a hot rush. I fought against clenching my thighs together when my channel throbbed.

Chapter Thirteen

LIAM

I sat beside Olivia and did my damnedest to keep from sliding my hand between her knees. Dinner with her had been divine. A distant corner of my mind kept nudging me with the persistent suggestion that what I was doing with Olivia wasn't anything of the usual sort when it came to women. I generally didn't take women on dinner dates, unless it happened by chance, such as I was out with my mates and we ended up at a restaurant and there were women there with us. It wasn't that I was opposed to the idea, but I'd simply never met a woman who inclined me to ask. Olivia had surprised me tonight. Oh, she had her moments of sternness, but it was as if she'd decided to cease worrying about whether it was proper to have dinner with me.

When she opened her door and I saw her curls tumbling wildly about her shoulders, I'd almost snogged her right then and there. She was such a tempting combination of beautiful and sexy, and she was so damn guileless that it made it all worse. My cock had been at half-mast all evening, the only time it wasn't was when I stumbled into the topic of her parents' death and my mum's. She was so refreshingly honest in her response. Outside of my own family, Alex and then Coach's comments about my mum, I barely spoke of it, yet somehow it had been okay with Olivia.

She shifted beside me, crossing and uncrossing her ankles, the subtle motion of her thigh under my palm knocking my mind right back to where we were—with Olivia pressed up against my side, her scent hinted with honey drifting around me, and her thigh warm under my touch. My need for her was so fierce, I truly didn't know if I could hold back much longer. I wanted to see and touch every inch of her and bury myself so deep inside that maybe I could slake the madness she elicited.

The automated speakers on the railcar announced her cross street. I reluctantly slid my palm off her leg and curled it around her hand as we stood. I hadn't considered this part of tonight. I was starting to realize I'd taken quite a lot for granted when it came to women. Usually, I didn't think about whether a woman might turn me away and leave me wanting. With Olivia, I did. As desperate as I was for her, my need was inextricably linked to hers matching mine. Speaking of things I'd never thought of with women, I had to admit I'd never wondered if a woman wanted me as much as I wanted her. But then, I'd never wanted a woman the way I wanted Olivia.

We stepped onto the sidewalk into the rain, which had surprisingly moved beyond a drizzle and was falling steadily now. Olivia paused to look up at me, and I was mesmerized. I stood there like a fool with rain falling all around us and stared down at her. Her lashes were damp and spiky, illuminating her eyes, so green I could lose myself in them. She had forgotten to pull her hood up and the raindrops falling on her hair gleamed from the soft glow of the streetlights.

A drop of rain rolled down her cheek, and I brushed it away with my thumb as I turned to face her. Her eyes searched my face. I didn't know what she saw there. All I knew was I had to taste her again. My eyes on hers to the last second, I dipped my head and fit my mouth over hers. The point of contact was electric, sending a bolt of lust through me. The contrasting heat of her lips to the chilly rain notched up the heat inside. A soft sound came from her throat as I threaded my hand into her damp curls and swept my tongue in her mouth.

I forgot everything but her—she was like a drug just for me, so sweet, so delicious and so intoxicating. She flexed in my arms and slipped a hand up behind my neck, her tongue tangling with mine. With the rain falling around us, I let go. With one hand tangled in her hair, I slid the other down her back and over the lush curve of her bottom. She'd worn this skirt that I was fairly certain had been designed solely to make me mad. It hugged her hips and I'd spent much of the evening wondering if I'd be able to tug it up and bury myself inside her. I pulled her against me, groaning in response to her moan and when she opened her thighs just enough for me to grind my cock into her.

A horn honked nearby, and Olivia tore her lips free with a gasp. Her eyes whipped up to meet mine. For a moment, I felt bereft, instantly missing the feel of her mouth under mine. I started to say something, but she spoke first.

"We're getting soaked. Come on." She stepped back and grabbed my hand. We ran through the rain together, dashing into the entrance to her building. She started to run up the stairs and paused on the bottom step, turning back to face me. Her eyes were dark and wild, her cheeks flushed and her skin damp from the rain.

"Would you like to come up?" she asked, her voice breathy.

Her question ranked right up there with some of the most unnecessary questions in the universe, but I loved that she asked it. At my nod, she spun away and all but dragged me up the stairs behind her. She lived on the third floor in this charming little building tucked amongst the more modern buildings in downtown Seattle. As such, we had two flights of stairs to climb. She came to an abrupt stop about halfway up the second flight, spinning back to me, her eyes wide and worried.

"Your knee! I'm so sorry. I forgot..." Her words trailed off, and she bit her lip, her eyes casting down to the knee in question.

"Is fine. Tim's had me on the stair-stepper every day all week."

Those gorgeous green eyes flicked back up. "Okay, I'll slow down though. I didn't mean..."

Our faces were close to level with her one step above me. I gave her hand a tug and slid my free hand down the curve of her hip, curling it around her bottom and pulling her close. "Hurry all you like, luv," I whispered right before our mouths collided again.

I wasn't much for snogging. It wasn't that I didn't take my sweet time and make sure any woman I was with walked away satisfied, it was more that I wanted to get to the main act, so to speak. But Olivia was different. I could have stood there on the stairs, damp from the rain and slightly chilled through, and kissed her for hours. The buttoned up doctor I'd met weeks ago abandoned all restraint once our lips were melded. Between long, wild tangles of our tongues, she nipped at my bottom lip and gasped when I slipped my hand around and tore her jacket open to fondle her breasts. She curled a leg around one of mine and arched into me, a low moan escaping into our kiss when I rolled a hard nipple between my fingers.

At the sound of footsteps starting up the stairs below us, I reluctantly pulled back. Her eyes were dazed, giving me some relief because I was about out of my mind and didn't want to be alone in this madness. She didn't seem to be aware of why I'd pulled back and curled a hand around my neck. "Upstairs, luv," I whispered against her lips. "We're about to have company."

Her eyes widened with alarm, and she turned, entirely forgetting about my knee again as she walked swiftly up the remaining stairs. Fortunately, my knee really was handling the stairs fine. We made it through the door and into her apartment. She released my hand and kicked off her shoes before striding away from me. I left my shoes beside hers by the coatrack and hung my jacket, while she turned up the heat and flicked a few lamps on, casting a soft glow about the cozy room. I liked her flat—it was small, but inviting with its warm colors and small sofa covered with pillows.

Olivia turned back in my direction as she peeled her raincoat off. I met her on her way across the room. Her coat fell to the floor when I stepped flush against her. I could barely think, much less act rationally, but I had to make sure of one thing.

"You'd best say so now if you'd like me to go." I closed my eyes and gulped in air. Opening them, I locked my gaze with hers. "I want you, Olivia, but I need to know if you want me too."

I could see the rapid flutter of her pulse in her neck, the flush cresting her cheeks, and feel her breasts rising and falling with her breath against my chest. She swallowed and lifted a hand to adjust her glasses. She was quiet long enough, I started to worry. Then, she nodded. When she didn't say anything, I was compelled to speak. "What does that mean?"

Her eyes widened, and she swallowed again. "I want you." Her words fell into the quiet room, crystal clear and soft.

A knot of tension I hadn't even known had been balled up in my chest eased. I reached up and removed her glasses, carefully setting them on a small table beside the couch. "Okay then."

I'd had all kinds of ideas about how I'd prove beyond any doubt to Olivia that sex wasn't boring. Most of them involved fantasies of how I'd be in control of myself because then I could orchestrate what was happening. I'd look back later and realize how little control I had and what a silly, arrogant man I'd been. The sound of her glasses clicking against the wood of the small table was like a fire alarm inside. I threaded my hand into her wild, dark curls and brought my lips to hers again. What followed was pure madness, my control lost in the wake of the lust pounding through me.

She sighed into my mouth, a soft sound coming from her throat, and I yanked her hard against me. It was as if our kiss on the stairs had been on pause. Her leg curled around mine and she arched into me. I could feel the tight peaks of her nipples through her thin blouse, and I shoved it up, groaning at the feel of her silky skin. Everything was in the way. I tore my mouth from hers and flung her shirt off. Those fumbled, heated, unplanned moments in her office hadn't given me time to truly look at her. I let my eyes travel down, tracing a finger around her taut nipples. She wore another flimsy excuse for a bra, the sheer cream lace offering glimpses of pink. I dragged my tongue over the lace, smiling against her when she moaned and arched into my mouth. While I poured my need to practically absorb her inside by drenching the lace covering her, I cupped both breasts in my palms, savoring the fullness. I finally lifted my head and almost came on the spot when I saw her.

Her eyes were half closed, her cheeks flushed and her breath coming in shallow pants. She was arching into me, rolling her hips against my cock, which was so hard it was a miracle I hadn't made a mess in my trousers. I dragged my tongue into the valley between her breasts and finally flicked my thumb under the clasp, groaning at the sight of her breasts tumbling free. They were perfect, her nipples wet, pink and standing erect. I couldn't help but suck one and then the other into my mouth again. When she gasped my name, I lifted my head. I didn't know why, but the sound of my name sent a whip of need through me.

"Yes, luv?"

Her eyes opened and narrowed. Without a word, her leg uncurled from where she'd hooked it behind mine. She reached between us and roughly tore my jeans open, sliding her hand over my cock. What little control I'd thought I had was lost, and I groaned, my forehead falling to hers and she curled her palm around me and stroked up and down over my briefs. My cock throbbed under her touch, and I needed more. Now.

Somehow we stumbled to her couch. That skirt I'd imagined slowly dragging up over her hips was tossed aside, along with the rest of our clothes in a fumbling mess. Suave was not the word I'd use to describe any of this. I was clinging to my control, hanging on with my fingernails. We ended up in a tangle on the sofa. I couldn't get enough of every inch and was busy exploring her with my lips and hands when she pushed me back. I dragged my eyes open, fuzzy and unfocused in my mind, to find her with that stern look. Oh God. I loved that look. Her eyes were narrowed. She pushed a finger on my chest.

"You need to be careful with your knee," she declared, her words crisp and bossy.

She was leaning back into the cushions, naked save for a pair of sheer black panties. Her breath was coming in gasps, and I could tell she was as bad off as me. My cock throbbed at the sight of her. I was stretched out over her, most definitely oblivious to my knee. "Dr. Bowen," I drawled. "So nice of you to make an appearance. My knee is quite fine, thank you."

I knew, I just knew, calling her doctor would elicit her proper side, the side that worried she shouldn't be with me. I wanted a flicker of that because I loved it so. Her lips tightened, her eyes fairly snapping. "I don't want you to do something stupid."

My lips had been mapping a path over the curve of her belly. I dipped my head and dropped another lingering kiss there before looking up again. "You're right. Give me just a minute and then I'll follow doctor's orders."

Her breath drew in sharply when I slipped my hand between her thighs and stroked across the silk there. It was wet, so wet. I dragged my fingers back and forth, lightly stroking the silk, savoring every roll of her hips and the low moan that escaped her. "Liam, it's not good for..."

I didn't wait to see what she might have to say and shoved the silk out of the way, finally getting to do what I'd been fantasizing about for weeks. I slid a finger into her channel, slick with the evidence of her need, and brought my mouth against her. Her hips bucked against me, and I settled in to taste her as thoroughly as I'd been wanting.

Chapter Fourteen

OLIVIA

Oh. My. God. I was going to melt into the couch. With the feel of Liam's fingers stroking into me and his tongue doing absolutely wicked things, I was drowning in need. Everything narrowed to my center, to a razor sharp knife-edge where I teetered until he swirled his tongue around my clit and sent me flying. I went taut and distantly heard my sharp cry as pleasure rippled through me. He slowly lifted his head and dragged his fingers out of me and yanked my underwear off with one swift tug. I was stunned as he trailed kisses up over my belly, lingering on my breasts before he stretched out over me. Somewhere along the way, need was already tightening its coil inside. The feel of his cock resting against my slippery folds nearly made me lose my mind all over.

A distant part of my brain tried to remember what I'd been saying before, well before Liam so thoroughly and emphatically disproved my long held belief that sex was boring and not worth the bother. His knee. That's it. I dragged my eyes open. "Your knee," I said weakly.

His eyes had gone navy, and I could feel his heart pounding against my breast. I knew he wanted me, as evidenced by the feel of every inch of his hot, hard length sliding against me as he arched his hips slightly. I clung to my sanity. It was all kinds of crazy to be here with him, but I truly couldn't allow him to endanger his recovery all because he made me lose my mind. "Tell me what I need to do about my knee...Dr. Bowen. But first, tell me if you're bored." His mouth curled at one corner in that grin of his that made my belly do flips inside.

I bit my lip to keep from laughing. I was half mortified because I knew he knew I was anything but bored. I shook my head.

"I want to hear you say it," he insisted, his grin widening.

"Okay. I'm not bored. At all," I said.

"Right then. So what am I to do about my knee?" he asked, his eyes glinting with mischief.

With my pulse pounding, a luscious shiver raced through me. I called on that part of me I knew so well— the doctor in me who focused on the mechanical functions of joints and things. "You shouldn't put too much pressure on it," I choked out when he rolled his hips into mine again.

I was so wet, it was almost ridiculous. His cock slid against me, coasting over the sensitive nub of my desire, the center of my entire world at the moment. I gasped, but I held onto a frayed thread of control.

"How do I make sure I don't put too much pressure on it?" he asked, his words tight.

I forced myself to move before I lost my mind all over again and shimmied out from under him. "Turn over," I said once I was standing.

My mouth went dry when he obeyed instantly. Dear God. His body was a work of art—all lean muscle, every inch of him defined. I'd seen him in bits and pieces, but just now was the first moment I had a chance to see all of him, and what a sight it was. He has a light dusting of dark hair on his chest that tapered down. I'd felt him against me and knew he was well-endowed, but the sight of him rock hard made me clench my thighs together.

His eyes on me, he reached a hand out and snagged his jeans from the messy pile of our clothes. In seconds, he was rolling a condom on and curling a palm around my calf. He slid his hand up my calf and thigh to curl around my bottom, giving it a squeeze before slipping his fingers between my thighs and stroking through my wet folds. The inside of my thighs were wet from my own need.

When I didn't move, he spoke. "Well luv, I turned over. Now what?"

He pushed himself up into the cushions slightly as he reached for me. I straddled him and settled my hips down, my eyes flying up when a low groan followed by a choked laugh came from him.

"If this is how I keep pressure off my knee, I'll do whatever you say."

I flushed and decided to tease him a little. I rocked my hips against him, savoring his groan. He gripped my hips and held me down, grinding into me and nearly making me come from just that. He loosened his grip, and I rose up. I needed to feel him inside me, needed it like I needed air to breathe.

"Olivia."

My eyes were down as I reached between us. I looked up to find his gaze—so hot and intense, I froze. The tip of his cock was right there, and I wanted to sink down so badly, but he gripped my hip and held me still.

"I want to see you," he said gruffly.

In slow motion, he eased his hold on me. I slowly sank down, locked in the web of his gaze, groaning at the feel of him filling me. It felt so good, so, so, so good. I held still when my hips met his with him seated deeply within me. My channel throbbed around him. Sex with Liam wasn't just parts fitting together. No, it was wild and raw and made me feel naked inside and out. I couldn't help myself and started to rock into him. We moved in slow motion, pleasure tightening and tightening inside, everything narrowing to the point of connection between us.

He slid his palm up my spine, subtly bringing me forward. My breasts pressed against his chest, as hard as the rest of him, as he whispered against my lips. "Come with me."

The sound of his crisp accent, rough with passion, was all it took to send me over when he rocked deeply into me. I cried out, my head falling into the curve of his neck. My channel clenched and tremors ran through me, the pleasure so acute I could hardly bear it. His arms wrapped around me, and he rocked his hips into me once more before he went taut, a rough cry escaping.

I stayed right where I was, breathing in the scent of his skin with pings of pleasure echoing through my body. He relaxed under me, and our breath slowed in unison. After a few moments, his palm stroked in slow passes up and down my spine. I didn't know what to do. I didn't want to move. Ever. I wanted to stay right here with Liam's arms around me, his cock deep inside of me, and this disarming intimacy shimmering around us.

"You're cold, luv."

His voice nudged me out of my dreamy state. I felt the goose bumps on my skin as his palm made another slow pass up my spine. I reluctantly lifted my head. I felt so exposed, it was hard to meet his eyes. His gaze was relaxed and warm and made my heart ease. I tried to think of what to say and was relieved when he spoke.

"Please tell me you're not planning to send me out in the rain now."

Considering I didn't want him to go anywhere ever, I shook my head immediately. I might not be comfortable with how I was feeling, but I was too close to what had just happened for reason to come online.

Though I hadn't said a word, Liam smiled slightly. "Right then. Shower."

Somehow we untangled ourselves and made it to the shower. He was completely comfortable in his nakedness, but then I expected he would be. Most athletes were as they spent plenty of time in locker rooms and were subject to the impersonal hands of trainers and the like. I was less so, which surprised me. Even though I'd considered sex boring before, I'd never been prudish. I supposed it was the intimacy of what happened that threw me. If he noticed, he ignored it. Once we were in the shower with steam billowing and hot water streaming over us, he slipped his hands around me from behind and dropped kisses on my neck. I had started to soap myself, and the soap fell to the shower floor with a thump.

"Liam," I said breathlessly.

"Mmm?"

"It's slippery in here. I don't want you to lose your balance."

My refuge was my doctor's mind.

He lifted his head and turned me in his arms. "I'll behave if you soap me off," he said with a grin.

Chapter Fifteen

LIAM

I awoke to the feel of Olivia's pliant, sleeping form nestled into me. I was curled up behind her, and she happened to wiggle her bottom against me, a rather effective way to wake me up in more ways than one. Her bed was a refuge of comfort as I'd discovered during the night. She had pillows galore and a silky down comforter paired with flannel sheets. I surmised I'd have slept ridiculously well even if we'd been under scratchy burlap because Olivia was beside me. My body was ready for another few hours of the many wonders of her, yet I was due at PT shortly.

I couldn't help but slide my hand over the curve of her hip and into the dip of her waist. She made a soft sound and shifted her legs. I had to brush her wild, tangled curls off her neck, so I could have a taste of her. Just one kiss, and then I'd roll over and drag myself out of bed, or so I told myself. Another sound from her—I'd never before been turned on by incoherent, sleepy mumblings, but every sound she made sent blood straight to my groin—and my lips made their way down to that soft curve where her neck met her shoulder. Goose bumps rose on her skin, and I smiled against her. She was awake. I could tell by the subtle tremor that ran through her body.

"Liam, what are you doing?" Her voice was husky from sleep, which only served to notch my need for her even higher. Sleepy and warm with her lush curves against me, she was the epitome of irresistible.

"Saying good morning," I replied as I reversed course and nibbled on her neck again.

I couldn't resist sliding my palm under the luscious curve of her breast and trailing my fingertips across her nipples, which obediently tightened the second I touched them. Her breath came out in a gasp as I slid my hand over her belly and into her curls, dipping my fingers into her folds. My entire body tightened at the slick wetness. "Liam..." she started to speak and then groaned when I stroked two fingers into her channel.

"Yes, luv?"

Sweet hell. She felt so good, every inch of her soaking my fingers and her channel clenching around me. Her only reply to my question was to roll her hips into my touch, simultaneously drawing me deeper inside of her and rubbing her bottom against my cock, which was so hard it's a miracle I didn't come right then. I needed to be inside of her. *Now*. I was about to sink into her when I realized I didn't have a condom anywhere near the bed.

As if she could read my mind, she reached a hand out to the night table by the bed, yanking the drawer open so hard she almost threw it to the floor. "Condom," she choked out in between gasps as she tossed the foil packet over her shoulder. Like lightning, I tore it open and smoothed it on. Her hair had fallen over her cheek. I brushed it back and curled around her, my lips, teeth and tongue making merry on her neck. With only a subtle shift, the head of my cock was positioned at her entrance.

I held still, barely able to restrain myself. "Olivia," I breathed.

Her eyes flickered open, and she turned her head just enough for me to lock onto her gaze. I was compelled by the need to see her face when I sank into her. Her cheeks were flushed and her hips rolled back into mine as I buried myself inside of her. My head fell into the curve of her neck, and I breathed in the scent of her. In contrast to the near desperate madness of last night, this was a slow dance into raw, dizzying bliss. I rocked into her wet, velvet clench, sinking deeper with each slow surge. Her skin was like silk, her scent like honeyed musk, and the soft sounds coming from her coiled me tighter and tighter inside, the pressure building to a crescendo. It snapped with a resounding jolt when her body tightened and her channel throbbed around my cock, a sharp cry breaking from her. My release thundered through me. I'd have likely fallen to the floor at the whiplash of it, so it was quite convenient to be curled around her in bed.

We lay still, and I found myself sifting through her silky curls. Aside from loving them for how wild and beautiful they were, I loved them even more for the way were the only hint of the Olivia I was coming to know underneath her prim exterior with her tidy professional outfits and her hair tamed into a bun. My phone buzzed, and I ignored it. It was probably Alex. He'd be making sure I was meeting him on time for practice. I didn't want to get up and leave this moment out of time.

Olivia wiggled her hips and rolled over, my cock sliding out of her warmth. Her eyes searched my face, and I wondered what she was thinking. A thread of anxiety wove inside of me. I wasn't used to this—this desire to linger, to do nothing more than *be* with someone. I pushed back against it, shoving the feeling away. She sat up, pulling the sheet up to cover herself as she did. I couldn't help but grin. Anything she did to be proper made me want to tease.

"Little late for that, wouldn't you say?" I asked.

Her cheeks flushed, and she tucked the sheet under her

armpits as she glared at me. She bit the inside of her cheek as she looked over at me.

Seeing as she didn't seem inclined to speak, I continued. "So, do you still think sex is boring, Dr. Bowen?"

Her cheeks went from flushed to fiery, her eyes darkened, and she leapt out of bed. I followed, albeit at a slower pace than I'd have liked. Mornings were when I was most aware of my still-recovering knee. It tended to be stiff and didn't loosen until I'd had a steaming hot shower. She appeared to be headed right where I needed to go, so I followed her into the shower, disposing of my condom on the way.

"What's a woman who declares sex boring doing with condoms by her bed?" I asked as I quickly soaped off and ran a hand down her back. I couldn't help but touch her. While I wasn't sure how long it would take me to sate myself with Olivia, just enough edge had been taken off for now that I could manage myself.

Olivia spoke through the water running over her face and hair as she turned. "Daisy gave them to me. In fact, she put them all over the apartment. I even found some in the kitchen once. She thought it would motivate me."

I tried not to laugh, but I couldn't stop it and had to lean against the wall to keep my balance. I finally opened my eyes to find Olivia glaring at me, hands on hips and eyes snapping.

I gulped in air and pushed away from the wall. "You just gave me a new challenge."

She cocked her head to the side. "Huh?"

"We have to find them all and use them."

I scrolled through the screen in front of me and mentally noted a few details before glancing up to the patient in front of me. A football player—of the American sort, a distinction I hadn't thought much of until Liam came along—sat in front of me on the exam table with a team doctor leaning against the wall behind him. This was a second opinion consult, and they'd flown the guy up here from Colorado. The player, Carl Taylor, looked weary and worried. He had good reason to be.

I set my computer tablet on the counter and clasped my hands over my knees. "Well Carl, let me get right to the point. As you know better than any of us, this is your second ACL tear. I think you can still play, but I need to be very clear about our limitations. If you choose to go forward with surgery, we can clean up the scar tissue built up there and do an entirely new graft. Our limits relate to the area where the old graft was attached and the care we need to take to make sure that area stays strong. I believe we can make things better, but what happens after that is up to you. I'm going to be very blunt—obviously you run hard when you play and you've struggled to modify the way you handle it when you're on the field and taking a hit. That's a big reason you've injured yourself more than once." I paused when Carl's brows rose.

He was clearly startled that I knew anything about how he played. "Right. I watch tape if I think it might help me understand the nature of your injury. I generally only do it for repeat injuries because it helps me know what we're dealing with and why. You're a defensive player, and I hear you're considered one of the best. When I reviewed the tapes from when you injured your knee, you were planted and your knee collapsed on the outside. Guess what that means?"

Carl sighed. "I need to not do that."

"Exactly. I can only imagine how hard it is because when you do something well, you instinctively keep doing that. If you choose to go forward with us treating you, I strongly recommend you set up video consults to work with our PT team after the surgery. For you to get back to playing, you need to be vigilant about changing some habits to keep from injuring your knee again."

Carl nodded and glanced to his team doctor who looked from Carl to me before nodding. "If you think it's doable, we're committed to whatever you recommend."

I'd already had my time to talk privately with Carl. He was still young and had a good ten years of play left in him if he could recover without reinjuring his knee again. I'd had consult cases like this where I turned them down, not because I didn't think we could help, but because of the player's attitude. Carl was open to any and all feedback, so I figured he had a shot of making this worthwhile. As I sat there looking over at him, Liam strolled into my thoughts—boldly, like he did everything. I marveled yet again at Liam's effect on me. Carl was handsome by any standards with his brown hair, blue eyes and body sculpted from stone. I felt nothing. Not even a tiny flicker of desire, not even when I tried to elicit it.

Yet, Liam had walked into this room, turned his gaze on me and set me afire inside and out. It was so bad, just thinking of him now and my channel throbbed with need. Oh hell. It was insane enough I'd crossed every conceivable boundary with a patient and put my job on the line, now I was getting hot and bothered about Liam in an appointment with another patient. I gave myself a sharp mental shake and focused on Carl, forcing my brain back onto the details of planning his surgery.

Later that evening, after a day of back to back appointments, I walked outside and paused on the sidewalk in front of the clinic. The clinic was situated on a street with just enough elevation to offer a view of Puget Sound. The sky was blessedly clear this evening, and the sun was setting over the water, the horizon ablaze in orange and red with the water shimmering under the colors. I took a deep breath and turned to walk home. A short walk later after I closed my apartment door and hung my jacket, I began to go into the kitchen to start a pot of tea. I paused by the sofa and looked around. My cozy apartment felt empty and quiet. One night, just one night, with Liam and he'd turned my world upside down. Aside from the swoon-worthy kisses and bone-melting sex, he was warm and funny, and against all reason, I liked him and enjoyed every minute of time with him.

I hadn't been able to help myself and looked him up online this morning. He, along with many soccer—correction football—stars, was a fixture in the gossip sites in Britain. I saw many photos of him with Alex and other players and only a few where he happened to be with a woman. According to the media, he had the reputation of hard-to-get. There was even a betting site with bets on when he might settle down with someone. There were a few recent stories that made my heart squeeze. As an attacking mid-fielder, otherwise known as a playmaker, he was relied upon for ball control and tactical awareness and the player who orchestrated the offense and distributed the ball—essentially the brain of the team. He was lauded as one of the best in the world and had led his last team in Britain to a league championship in his first year. There were numerous articles savaging him for losing his focus in the last few games he'd played and speculating as to whether his mother's death had contributed to the problem. I wanted to scream at them because of course it did! It shouldn't matter so much that he couldn't be human and stumble a bit in his grief for his mother.

I looked around my small apartment and wondered what Liam saw in me. I might be a good surgeon and didn't doubt my intellectual strength, but to think a man like him who was drooled over worldwide might want me was a bit of a stretch. To say it was hard to believe was an understatement. The weekend had gone by with me managing to keep from giving into the burning urge to see him again. He'd texted me regularly and appeared to be planning to ask to see me every day until I gave in again. I just didn't know if it was the wisest thing to do. Yet, here in this moment, I ached to see him.

Restless, I spun on my heel and snagged my phone out of my purse where I'd dropped it on the floor. I quickly texted Daisy.

Dinner?

Her reply was swift. *Where?*

That Thai place. Forget what it's called.

Daisy and I had dined in Seattle all through college and med school, so she knew exactly what I meant despite my vague response.

Meet you there in 30!

———

Almost precisely thirty minutes later, I walked into the Thai restaurant, the sign reminding me of its name, Thai Paradise. Daisy stood by the reception desk and gave a small wave. Her blonde hair was pulled into a loose braid, which swung when she leaned over to pull me in for a hug. "It's so perfect you texted! They said three minutes and our favorite corner table will be ready." She idly twirled the end of her braid and looked over at me. "I bet you had a better day than me."

"Why do you say that?"

"Queen Mean called me in to give me shit for not being promotional enough with one of our new studies."

Queen Mean was the bane of Daisy's existence at her job that she otherwise loved. As a medical researcher fresh out of med school, she was at the bottom of the ladder in her field. She was brilliant and had easily landed a position at a research facility, but she had to deal with a few egos—one of them being Queen Mean who wasn't a doctor but wished she was. From what I understood, she focused too hard on trying to push medication trials out the door too soon. With all the hubbub over bad press in that very area, you'd think she had more sense. Daisy was true blue when it came to digging into the nitty gritty of research, so she was endlessly patient with the process of medical trials.

"She's a bitch and she's intimidated by you," I declared firmly. "She also hates that the boss you share with her respects the hell out of you."

Daisy looped her arm through mine and squeezed. "See, I already feel better."

The waitress waved to us from the corner, and Daisy promptly dragged me to the table. Once we were seated, we chatted casually while our waitress got us drinks and took our order. After we were settled in and I was mid-sip, Daisy almost made me spew tea on the table.

"So, I happened to be driving by your building Sunday morning on the way to the gym and saw Liam leaving your building. What was Mr. Hottie doing at your place at that hour?"

With tea dribbling down my chin, I snagged a napkin and wiped it off. Daisy driving by my place was perfectly normal. We'd joined the very gym she mentioned together in med school. We occasionally managed to meet there, but we'd both gotten so busy with work since we graduated, it was more challenging to coordinate our schedules. I wasn't used to anyone noticing anything about my personal life because there wasn't anything to notice. I looked over at her and sighed, feeling torn. I wanted to tell her everything, yet I was all a muddle about the potential professional disaster I'd stumbled into. Even worse, I didn't know how to handle the depth of my feelings for Liam. If there was anyone who could help me get some perspective, it was Daisy, so I forged ahead. "You might be happy to know those condoms you left all over the place finally came in handy," I said.

Daisy's mouth dropped open for a second and then she let out a whoop. "Oh my God! This is so awesome! You *finally* decide to have some fun, and he's just so delicious." She leaned back and clapped her hands softly. "Okay, tell me everything."

Daisy was my oldest friend, so I generally did tell her everything. In fact, I'd complained at length about how boring my past sexual exploits had been. With both of us being doctors and going through med school in tandem, we were also far more accustomed to discussing topics that would make others blush. Yet, for reasons I couldn't fathom, telling her everything just now felt strange. What happened with Liam was so intense, so startling in its intimacy, I didn't know how to talk about it. Yet, I certainly wasn't about to leave her in the dark because I was stumbling and fumbling for how to handle my feelings.

With my cheeks hot, I adjusted my glasses and met her gaze, trying to shove my uncertainty aside. "Well, he took me to dinner..."

"Where?" she jumped in.

"13 Coins."

Daisy's eyes widened. She knew how much time I'd spent there with my parents because she'd gone along with us many times before they died. She also knew it was their anniversary restaurant. "Whoa. That's kind of, well, meaningful."

I started winding a napkin around my index finger. "Maybe. Liam obviously didn't know anything about the place." Because I was uncomfortable with even thinking about that, I pushed ahead. "Anyway, so we had dinner and then, well, he spent the night."

Daisy's eyes searched my face. "Are you okay?"

I shrugged, my chest tightening with a small knot of anxiety. I didn't know if I was okay. Was it okay to miss Liam as much as I did when we'd only spent one night together? Was it okay for me to wish he were someone other than an internationally famous footballer who was listed in betting books for reasons that had nothing to do with sports? Was it okay to suddenly rethink all of my preconceived notions about men and relationships and wish for something I'd never wanted? Was it okay that my body was so attuned to anything about Liam that all I had to do was think of him and heat slid through my veins, butterflies amassed in my belly, and my panties got wet? For example, right now.

With those questions tumbling through my mind, I looked over to find Daisy's warm brown eyes on mine. "Oh," she said softly. "You like him, I mean, you *really* like him. Don't get so stressed about it. He really likes you too. I could tell."

"How could you tell?" I asked, nearly breathless for her answer and wondering what to do about how much her answer mattered to me. I wasn't prone to breathlessness over, well, anyone. I didn't enjoy being tossed like a kite in the winds of my emotions.

At that moment, our food arrived. I'd chosen a red curry chicken with cashews, while Daisy had gone for drunken noodles. Once our waitress departed again, I looked over at

Daisy. She took a bite of food and held her chopsticks up while she chewed. After a swallow of water, she leaned back. "Just the way he looked at you. It's not like I know him well, but there's those looks that are all about sex and then the looks that are more. His was more."

I took a deep breath and let it out with a sigh. "I think I've completely lost my mind."

Daisy grinned. "Nah. You're human. I always knew you had it in you, I just wondered who might get under your skin."

I stared at Daisy, that uncertainty I was trying so hard to beat back rising inside again. Everything I was feeling startled me so. Unable to think clearly, I swatted my confusion away and rolled my eyes. "Fine. So what should I do?"

"See him as much as you can," Daisy said with a firm nod. "I mean, he's so easy on the eyes you might as well get every minute you can. I'm getting the idea you're not going to give me any details since you skipped right over that, but I'm guessing he wasn't boring in bed." Her sly smile sent another rush of heat up my cheeks.

"Definitely not."

"I'll stop by your place tomorrow and make sure you're stocked up on those condoms."

I burst out laughing. When I managed to stop, I shook my head. "We only used one of yours and you left them everywhere last time."

"Yeah, and you threw away half of them."

Conversation started to move on, but I had one more worry I couldn't seem to shake. "Do you really think it's okay that I did this with a really, really recent patient?"

"Former patient. It's been weeks since his surgery, and he's officially no longer your responsibility," Daisy said between bites, waving her chopsticks in the air for emphasis.

"Right, but…"

Daisy shook her head empathically. "Oh stop it! Moving on. Bradley at work offered us tickets to a Stars game. I was thinking we should go together. You could see Liam play and I can ogle the rest of the team. Whaddya think?"

"Liam won't be playing for a while, but it'd be fun to go anyway. Shouldn't you go with Bradley? I mean, they're his tickets."

"Bradley'll be there, but he has four tickets, so I figure it's maybe you, me and Harper."

"You sure Bradley wants a group date?"

Bradley was Daisy's 'friends with benefits' friend. I was never quite sure how to interpret what that meant.

Daisy shrugged. "I know it doesn't make sense to you, but we really are just friends. If he cared about whether I brought anyone with me, he certainly wouldn't have offered up the tickets. Plus, Liam should be back to playing by then. It's for a game over three months out. Those tickets sell like wildfire and it's all because of Liam and the other players they signed from London. The Stars finally have a real chance."

The idea of seeing Liam play sent my belly in a somersault. This should have knocked some sense into me. Although most of my surgeries involved professional athletes, it was safe to say I didn't feel too passionate about sports of any kind. It was more of a clinical interest, a curiosity about how the body worked and what was necessary for a particular player to play in peak form. It was all about getting them back to their best. Those screaming fans —not me. But the thought of watching Liam in action sent a hot shiver up my spine.

Chapter Seventeen

LIAM

I stepped off the treadmill and snagged the towel hanging on the handlebar, wiping my face and draping the towel over my shoulder. Tim stepped off the treadmill beside me, his eyes traveling up and down my body. Being a professional athlete had me accustomed to constant perusal in an impersonal sense by coaching staff and the like.

"How's the knee feeling?" he asked.

I flexed my knee and leaned my weight on it. "Great, actually. Honestly, the only time I notice much difference anymore is right when I get out of bed. Takes a minute to loosen up." It was going on a month since my surgery, which amazed me when I thought about it. If it weren't for my near obsession with Olivia, I surmised the time would be dragging, yet she gave me plenty to think about. I was also busy with PT, attending team meetings and observing practices. I might be a bit restless, but I wasn't bored.

I grabbed the water bottle Tim handed over and guzzled most of it down. I'd just put in a good thirty minutes on the combo treadmill he had me using daily. He'd gradually begun to up the intervals, adding more intensity to the workout. This was only one part of what we did daily. I spent so much time with Tim, I'd gotten to know him quite well. I thanked the stars I liked the guy, otherwise these would be some long days.

Tim gestured for me to follow him over to another part of the gym in the clinic. They had an entire area filled with pulleys and whatnot to build strength. Football, at least the kind I played, didn't necessitate the bulk American football players needed, so I wasn't buried in the weights section like a few others working out at the clinic. I was starting to get impatient to be back in play. But I'd quickly discovered following Tim's recommendations seemed to be working like a charm, so I hewed to his plodding pace.

I was in the middle of some stretches, when Tim paused what he was saying when someone said his name. At the sound of Olivia's voice, a prickle ran up my spine and a smile bloomed inside and out. Every so often the surgeons passed through the workout area, yet this was the first time Olivia had been in here when I was. I slowly stood from where I'd been seated on the mats and turned to see her walking in our direction. Her eyes widened slightly when she saw me. It had been almost a week since I'd seen her, what with her side-stepping me every time I tried to persuade her to see me again. My body tightened at the memory of the last time I had seen her—buried deep inside of her with her pulsing around me. Oh yes, that had been one of the best mornings I'd ever had, following one of the best nights.

She was wearing a skirt again, a narrow, fitted skirt that came to her knees. A perfectly respectable skirt, nothing even the slightest bit naughty about it. All I could think about was the last time I saw her in perhaps that very same skirt with it shoved up around her thighs and my fingers stroking into her slick channel. As before, she wore a simple blouse over the skirt, buttoned as far as it could go without choking her, and a white lab coat. She must be in consult mode today, instead of seeing patients for surgery.

She stopped in front of us and reached up to adjust her glasses. Her curls were tightly pulled back with only one wild curl escaping and tangling around her glasses. Tim rested his hands on his hips. "Dr. Bowen, what brings you here?"

"I need a few minutes to check in about the surgery from yesterday morning. He's scheduled to meet with you tomorrow afternoon. I'm booked for the rest of today, so I wanted to make sure we scheduled a time to meet before you see him."

"Of course. Let me check my schedule," Tim replied, pulling his smartphone out of his pocket. I assumed he was checking his calendar.

Olivia's eyes flicked to me, the first time she actually looked at me since she reached us. The moment our gazes connected, it was as if a match lit the air between us. My cock hardened, and a subtle flush rose on her cheeks.

"Hello Dr. Bowen," I said with a wink and almost burst out laughing when the flush on her cheeks deepened to cherry red. I figured my best bet was to behave as I usually would, and I loved to flirt. Tim would think nothing of it.

She adjusted her glasses again and swallowed audibly. "Hello Liam. It looks like you're recovering quite nicely."

Tim glanced up from his phone. "He's doing great. He's definitely on track to meet our goal of getting him back in action within three months." He tapped his phone. "Let's check in tomorrow first thing. Will 7:30 work for you?" he asked, looking to Olivia.

She nodded and started to say something. I knew she'd likely move right along after that, so I cut in. "Dr. Bowen, I meant to ask something." She snapped her mouth shut, her eyes narrowing on me. I loved it when she looked all proper and annoyed with me. The air around us fairly crackled with the tension emanating from her and damn did it turn me on.

"I've been doing some reading to make sure I can move things along. I understand I might need to be careful about putting pressure on my knee. Can you clarify what that means? Does it relate to my actual playing or...?" I let my words trail off. I'd just bloody lied about reading anything of the sort, but I wanted to tease Olivia. She'd insisted on riding me the other night, all because she didn't want me to put any pressure on my knee. She could ride me to madness again and again if it meant I was buried deep inside of her.

She shifted her legs, and the flush on her cheeks deepened. If I hadn't been so attuned to her, I might not have noticed that she rubbed her thighs together, making me wonder if she was as wet as I was hard. Her eyes flicked to Tim, but he was distracted and texting something on his phone. Her gaze swung back to me, her cheeks still cherry red. "Not knowing what you were reading, I can't speak specifically to that. Generally speaking, pressure on your knee would come from extending it too much in this healing stage, or actual pressure, such as kneeling on it," she finally said.

"Ah. Well that's helpful. I'll be certain to be careful about that." I almost grinned because it was so fun to tease her, yet I'd put myself in a bad state with wanting her so badly just now. I needed to ease up if only not to make a fool of myself.

Tim glanced up and slipped his phone back in his pocket. "Sorry about the interruption there." He glanced between us, his eyes narrowing slightly. "Did you need anything else?" he asked, his question directed to Olivia. "If not, we'll get back to work."

"That was all. Thank you." Olivia held still for a moment before giving her head a little shake and turning away. I watched her hips sway with her steps under her tidy, proper skirt and thought again about yanking it up and bending her over.

After she exited the room, Tim cleared his throat. I had

lost track of time and felt a little lost myself. Olivia did that to me. Tim's words startled me.

"Dr. Bowen is one of the best surgeons here and one of the nicest people I know. Seeing the way you're looking at her, I'm going to flat out tell you I'll personally kick your ass if you hurt her. She's not a woman to tease with," Tim said bluntly.

I met his gaze head on, trying to control my expression even though he'd startled me. I considered what to say. I was coming to learn my life was now divided. There was 'before Olivia' time and 'after Olivia' time. Before Olivia, I'd have shrugged and carried on, easily letting go of any fantasies I had. Easy come, easy go. After Olivia, I wondered how to make sense of the jumble of feelings swirling inside me. I couldn't even fathom hurting her, but then what the bloody hell did that mean? I *loved* teasing her, but not the way he meant. I knew I couldn't tell him what had transpired between us. I didn't think Tim would care for the reasons Olivia thought, but I knew it would bother her, so I wouldn't say a word. I called upon my usual swagger and shrugged, aiming for casual. "Just enjoying the view."

Tim arched a brow. "Fair enough, but cut it out. Dr. Bowen won't appreciate it."

No. No, she most certainly wouldn't and didn't...unless we were alone. I shrugged again and got back to my stretching.

A few hours later when the sky was turning wispy gray and the streetlights flickered on as I walked the few blocks to my apartment, I stopped on the sidewalk and slipped my phone out. I'd tried to find Olivia as I was leaving the clinic, but her office was dark and I didn't trust myself to try to find her in the examination area. Our brief encounter in the gym had sent my body into hours of longing and lust. Much as I didn't give a bloody damn if anyone saw us together, I knew she did, and I respected that.

I pulled her number up and texted her.

I'm not above groveling if that's what's required to see you again.

I leaned against the building closest to me and watched the busy street as I waited to see if she'd reply. When I felt my phone vibrate in my pocket, I pulled it out.

Don't be so dramatic. How about tomorrow?

Tonight. Please.

I stared at the screen, waiting impatiently as the dots blinked at me, indicating she was typing.

Okay. In an hour. Where?

Your place to start. Leave your hair up.

I'd abandoned any sense within myself and freely admitted I loved her hair. I especially loved seeing it all tidy and then making it wild and messy.

Are you serious?! It's my hair.

And I love it. See you in an hour.

I didn't wait to see if she had anything to add and pushed off the building to stop by my flat first.

Within moments, I walked into the flat I shared with Alex and headed straight for my room. I'd showered at the clinic, but figured perhaps I could bother to change. Alex gave a wave from where he sat on the couch watching game tapes. I quickly changed and returned to the living room, plunking down beside him on the couch. I glanced at the screen and almost flinched. He was watching one of the games we lost back in London. I knew the team we'd lost to was scheduled to play our new team here in Seattle for an exhibition game, so it made perfect sense for him to watch. The Stars had yet to play this team, so we didn't have the option to watch prior matches. The only reason they were playing was for the press. American pro teams didn't play British pro teams unless it was for exhibition. It was painful to try to watch. I'd been so bloody out of it. Mum's death had thrown me for a loop of the worst sort. I watched as I missed the critical pass that allowed the opposing team to steal the ball.

Alex hit pause and glanced to me. "How'd PT go today?"

"Good, I guess. Tim thinks I'm on track to be back in play on time."

Alex held my gaze and nodded slowly. "Good. You're not too gimpy," he said with a slow grin.

I punched him lightly in the shoulder. "Not so much." I nodded toward the frozen screen. "Think the team's ready for those blokes?"

Alex ran a hand through his hair and leaned back into the couch. "Think so. We need you though. Matt's doing his best, but he's not you."

Alex was referring to Matt Brady, the backup player for my position on the team. I liked Matt, and he was a solid player. I wasn't much for rating my skills against a teammate, but I knew Matt didn't play at the level I did. My chest tightened and that anxiety I'd thought mostly banished rose inside. It was impossible not to wonder if I'd make it back to form and be able to play the way I had before. With my PT progress, I felt good, but I had enough sense to know I wouldn't know until I was back in play. I took a slow breath and tried to push the anxiety away. "Right. He's got some solid skills. He can get the team through this patch if you guys make some adjustments."

Alex nodded. "Right. Working on it." He paused to take a long pull from the beer he had sitting on the coffee table. "Where you headed?" he asked when he set his beer down again.

"Dinner with Olivia." Alex wasn't too nosy for a mate, but it was pointless to hide much from him. He knew me too bloody well.

He held my gaze for a long moment and nodded slowly. "Since when do you take a girl out more than once?"

"Since Olivia," I said simply.

He chuckled softly. "Right, mate. Here I was worried about her and now I'm wondering if I need to worry about you."

I shifted my shoulders and eyed him. "No need to worry, mate."

Alex arched a brow, but he didn't add anything. I ignored the thread of discomfort rising inside. There was 'before Olivia' and 'after Olivia,' and I hadn't a clue how to navigate the disquieting feelings swirling inside.

Chapter Eighteen

OLIVIA

I glared at the mirror after another failed attempt to make my curls behave. Liam had asked me to leave my hair up, and I'd proceeded to spend close to a half hour dallying with my hair. First, I decided I was going to leave it down out of spite. It got under my skin to have him tell me what to do with my hair. Yet, it turned me on, sweet hell did it turn me on. So then, I decided I'd put it back up. I wore my hair in a knot almost every day, so this should have taken me no more than a few minutes. My hair was being naughty and fighting every attempt to tame it. I never should have taken it down. There was this one curl that kept popping out every which way. I ran my hand under the water and smoothed the curl into place, knowing full well it would likely unwind itself as soon as it dried.

At the sound of a knock on the door, I realized I hadn't even had time to change. I was still wearing my plain black skirt and cream colored blouse from work—both nothing but boring and professional. Well, hell. I didn't have time to do anything about it, so I walked to the door and opened it. Liam was leaning inside the doorframe, one hand in his pocket pulling the waistband of his jeans down just enough to reveal a glimmer of his skin with that oh-so-tempting area where his muscled abs tapered down. My breath caught when I looked up into his deep blue eyes. His black hair gleamed under the soft lights from the hall, and his mouth curled into a slow smile.

"Hello luv."

It felt as if the very air around us heated. My belly turned in a slow flip, and my pulse took off. Somehow I managed to speak. "Hi. I, um, haven't had time to change," I said, gesturing to my skirt. "If you can wait a few minutes, I'll..."

"No need to change. I *love* when you look all proper and such."

I was instantly wet. When I realized my mouth had fallen open, I snapped it shut and spun away from the door. "Do you have to say proper like that?" I asked as I all but stomped over to grab my purse. I didn't much feel like bothering to change because all I'd do was obsess over it, but still.

When I turned back to the doorway, Liam was standing right where I'd left him. "How shall I say proper?" he asked.

I slid my arms into my jacket and draped my purse over my shoulder. "Not like that," I said, exasperated with his question.

He arched a brow, the hot look in in his eyes nearly melting me on the spot. "As soon as you tell me the proper way to say proper, I'll be happy to oblige," he replied, dragging the emphasis out on the word in question.

His crisp British accent sent flutters twirling in my belly. No one had ever warned me against speaking to men with British accents. Right about now, I wished they had because all Liam had to do was speak, and the sound of his voice made me feel wild and restless inside.

Somehow I managed to walk down the stairs, ignoring the wet heat between my thighs. Every step served to subtly rub my slick folds together, sending little jolts of pleasure through me. This was pure madness. Walking, *walking,* was a problem when it came to Liam.

I hadn't even thought about where we were going. When we stepped out into the soft darkness, Liam glanced to me. "Where are we going?" he asked.

"I hadn't thought about it. Any preferences?" Habit alone got me through the niceties.

"Luv, I've only been in Seattle for a bit. A few of the other players from here have dragged me and my mates out and about, but I can't say I have any suggestions. We could go to 13 Coins again."

Most days, I'd agree to go to 13 Coins, yet it felt too close to home in more ways than one. I could barely get a grip on my body and entwining memories with Liam at a place that held so many other memories connected to my parents didn't seem like the best idea. I thought quickly. "How about Thai food?"

Just as he nodded, the light rail came to a smooth stop at the cross street. I grabbed his hand. "Come on."

A short ride later, we stepped off the railcar and Liam walked alongside me, his palm resting in the curve of my back. The heat of his touch sifted through my jacket and blouse. I'd brought him to the same place Daisy and I had eaten earlier in the week. Though Seattle was awash in restaurants, I hewed to the tried and true. The waitress grinned when she saw me, her eyes flicking an appreciative glance in Liam's direction.

Once we were seated, Liam looked over at me. "Okay, luv. You order for me."

I adjusted my glasses. "Are you sure?"

He nodded firmly. "Yup. I've only had Thai once before."

Our waitress arrived and quickly took our order. After I asked her to give Liam some suggestions, he grinned as soon as she suggested drunken noodles. "Oh, that's rich. Drunken noodles sound as if they were made for me."

A bit later, our waitress had cleared out plates and was

bringing an after dinner glass of wine. As I'd have expected, Liam was charming and funny throughout dinner. He regaled me with tales of practical jokes he and his teammates played on each other back with his team in Britain. I could tell he missed his old team and realized his time with the Seattle Stars had been brief before his injury. Given that he'd been a central acquisition for the team and held a leadership role, I could only imagine he was facing some challenges with the adjustment and having to sit on the sidelines right now.

Our wine arrived, and Liam glanced over after I'd taken a rather generous sip. "Well, was it so bad, luv?" he asked with a wink.

"Was what so bad?"

"Seeing me. You've been avoiding me like the plague."

My spine straightened. "I have not!" A complete lie, but I wasn't quite up to discussing aloud why I'd been avoiding him.

His blue eyes darkened and coasted over me, sending a hot shiver through me with my skin heating everywhere his eyes landed. "Oh yes you have. You haven't figured out yet that only makes me want you more. I love a challenge," he murmured.

Our table was in a corner and about as tiny as a table could get and leave room for two people to eat. His knees had been bumping against mine throughout dinner. I jumped a little when I felt his hand curl over my bare knee and slide up my thigh. I took a gulp of wine and wondered if I'd made a serious miscalculation. I'd been avoiding Liam because I had no idea how to handle any of this. Despite Daisy's declaration that I should enjoy as much of him as I could, I didn't know if that was a good idea. Because I liked him too much, and when I was with him, I couldn't turn away. Being with him was like the sun parting the clouds after days of rain. The feel of it on one's skin was so divine.

Liam made me want things I'd never even considered. Yet, my position was so precarious with him. There was the sticky issue of him being a quite recent patient, and then the fact of his near rock star sports status. I was nothing more than a small-town girl who'd ended up in his orbit because I was brainy enough to sail through med school and land the job of my dreams. I shouldn't wonder the things I wondered about him. Such as, how it would feel for this to be more than a surreal connection? What did he really think about me? And did he want me the way I wanted him? Was he nearly out of his mind with need whenever we were close?

My breath came out in a hiss when he reached the juncture between my thighs. His palm stayed right where it was, curled over my thigh with his thumb softly stroking back and forth. My entire being narrowed to the small strip of flesh where his touch moved in a slow sweep. "Liam, what are you doing?" I asked in a fierce whisper.

My cheeks were hot, hell, my whole body was hot, and it was a miracle I didn't dissolve into a puddle in my chair.

His eyes met mine, the blue gone dark as navy. "Touching you," he said, the low timbre of his voice sending a ripple of need through me.

Right then, he slid his palm down the curve of my inner thigh where my skin was so sensitive. I didn't even realize I was widening my thighs until I felt my skirt slide up further. He trailed a finger over the wet silk there. I was drenched with my own arousal as he commenced to tease me to madness right there in the restaurant where his hand was hidden under the table in the dark corner. All he did was drag his fingers back and forth, coasting over my swollen clit again and again and again. My breath came in short pants, and I almost forgot where we were. His eyes were on me the entire time, and I couldn't tear my gaze free—locked in this sensuous, shimmering web of desire with him. He slipped a finger under the edge of my panties and sank it knuckle deep into my channel. I was dripping wet, and he slid home instantly. My hips were rolling into his touch, and I was on the verge of a climax, small ripples of pleasure building inside.

I was snapped out of the madness when the waitress came out of the kitchen entrance nearby, the swinging door banging shut behind her and nudging me into awareness. I clamped my knees together. "Oh my God! We have to stop."

His hand was effectively trapped between my thighs now. He arched a brow and eased his finger in another slow stroke. "Must we now?" he asked, his tone hinted with that haughtiness.

The raw desire pounding through me combined with mortification made me hot all over. I glared at him. "Yes!"

Our waitress was making her way back across the restaurant from delivering a tray of food to a table on the far side of the room, and I could tell she was aiming right for us. "Ease up, luv," Liam said softly.

I relaxed my knees, and he slipped his fingers out of me. He carefully put the silk back where it belonged and threw a grin at me just as the waitress reached our table. The heat of his touch disappearing sent a pang of longing through me. That's how out of my mind I was. I might've been mortified at almost tumbling into an orgasm in a restaurant, yet that didn't stop me from wanting his fingers shoved right back inside of me.

I managed to nod along and speak a few words while the waitress checked to see if we needed anything else, but my attention was focused elsewhere. Specifically on Liam and when we'd be alone. I had no idea how much time passed between then and when we found our way outside. I was only vaguely aware of my surroundings. It had started to rain softly since we'd entered the restaurant a few hours ago. The feel of his hand on my low back was searing. Liam hailed a cab, and I didn't even think to question why. I almost never took cabs. Once we were in the backseat with the panel up between us and the driver up front, Liam yanked me onto his lap.

My knees fell apart as I caught my balance and instantly sank down against him, savoring the feel of his hard shaft through the layers of my panties and his jeans. He leaned back and lifted his hands, reaching to untie my hair. With a flick, the elastic snapped off and landed God-knows-where in the cab. My curls unwound and spilled over my shoulders. He ran his hands through them before sliding one hand to cup the back of my head and leaning in to kiss me. Our mouths collided in a hot, wet and overpowering kiss. I couldn't get close enough fast enough and wound my arms around him, plastering my body against his.

I sighed into his mouth at the feel of him—all hard muscles with warmth emanating like a furnace. He groaned into my mouth when I rolled my hips against him, almost crying out at the sweet streak of pleasure from the pressure of his hard cock against me. With a muttered swear, he tore his lips free. His eyes locked with mine in the dim light of the cab, his gaze so intense, my heart gave a hard kick. It felt as if we were alone in the world, protected in the quiet of the cab with cars rolling by and the soft patter of the rain on the roof. The air around us was heavy with the weight of desire, taut with need, and that intimacy I didn't know how to comprehend hung around us. When I was with him like this, none of my worries about us mattered. All I knew was it felt so good, I felt held and protected in his embrace. It was so much more than just sex.

Liam swallowed, drawing my eyes down, and I could see the rapid beat of his pulse along the column of his throat. His hand sifted through my curls, and he subtly arched his hips, sending another sharp spike of pleasure scoring through me.

He freed his hand from my curls and traced it down over my shoulder, lingering along the curve of my breast before moving to unbutton my blouse, so swiftly it was hanging open and the cool rush of air sent goose bumps prickling over my skin.

I became vaguely aware of where we were. "Liam, maybe we shouldn't…"

"Tell me everything we shouldn't do, luv. I shall have to do all of it," he said with a low chuckle.

I couldn't help but smile. He was so naughty, and I secretly loved it. I leaned back and looked at him. He rolled a taut nipple between his thumb and forefinger, the thin silk of my bra sliding back and forth heightening his touch. "Shall I not do this?" he asked in a gruff whisper.

Wordless, I shook my head.

"I think…" He dragged his hand over the curve of my belly. I experienced a pang of self-consciousness. I'd never been one of those thin girls, and I loved good food too much to deprive myself. As such, I had the curves to show it. He glanced down and my eyes followed his gaze. My skirt had ridden up around my thighs and the silk of my black thong was visible against the obvious bulge in his jeans. He gave my generous hip a squeeze. "Have I mentioned I love every inch of you?" he asked in a murmured, instantly dissolving my pang of insecurity.

His eyes flicked up to catch mine, right as he dragged his fingers across the wet silk between my thighs. I was beyond shame at this point and couldn't keep from rolling my hips into his touch. "I think we need to finish what we started before we get you home."

Instead of worrying about where we were, I was worried he meant to finish this here when I couldn't even bear the idea of him not coming home with me. "No! We can wait. I want to…"

"Oh luv. There will be plenty more. Think of this as an appetizer. I know just what I want to do when we get back to your flat, and it won't work in here."

He pushed my panties out of the way and sank two fingers inside of me. Between the long, slow tease he'd put me through in the restaurant and the last few minutes, I was so close to ready, I almost came instantly. He tangled his free hand in my curls again and fit his mouth over mine. With his tongue mimicking the stroking of his fingers in my channel, my climax burst through me, my cries caught in the heat of our kiss.

I tipped my forehead against his as he slowly eased away from our kiss. My breath came in rough gusts, and I tried to pull myself together, but I was nearly limp from the climax that had rocked me. When I finally managed to lift my head and open my eyes, I met his gaze and my heart set to pounding again. The need in his eyes was so raw and so intense, it hit me right in my chest.

Chapter Nineteen

LIAM

Somehow, bloody hell if I knew how, I managed to help Olivia button her blouse. She didn't move from my lap until the cab rolled to a stop in front of her building. I was so wracked with need, I could barely think. All I knew was I needed to be inside of her and needed every inch of her bared to me. A distant voice in the far reaches of my mind tried to warn me I was in way over my head. I was so far gone over Olivia, I couldn't even stop to think, much less listen to that part of me that thought I'd gone and lost my mind. Because I had, well and truly.

The driver slid the panel open and called out the fare. I was stumped for a moment, my brain so muddled I couldn't comprehend, and then fumbled for my wallet to pay him. Somehow we stumbled out of the cab. Olivia smoothed her skirt down and held her jacket together, covering her crookedly buttoned blouse. The soft rain fell in cool spikes against my cheeks, just barely easing the hot lust pounding inside of me. I looked down at her with her curls a wild halo around her face and her gorgeous green eyes glowing under the streetlights. My need for her was so fierce I was almost shaking from it. I curled my hand around hers and cleared my throat.

"Shall we?" I asked, my voice almost croaking as I gestured to the entrance to her building.

She gave her head a little nod and turned, tugging me along behind her. She dropped her keys by the door, but then we made it through. I couldn't keep my eyes off the sway of her hips as she climbed the stairs ahead of me. I called on every ounce of discipline I had not to take her right here in the stairwell. In a daze, I followed her into her flat. She hung her jacket on a coatrack by the door, gesturing for me to do the same. After she slipped her shoes off, I followed suit while she walked across her small flat to turn up the furnace. I met her halfway across the room, sliding my hands over the lush curves of her hips. Her breath caught, and her eyes slammed to mine.

I'd had this idea we'd get back to her apartment, and I'd seduce her all over again slowly. But I was way too far gone for that. My cock was so hard, I was on the verge of losing control without laying another finger on her. We happened to be standing right beside the sofa. I'd like to say I planned it that way, but it was solely because her flat was rather small.

"Turn around," I said gruffly.

Her dark green gaze held mine for a beat and then she turned. I stroked one hand through her hair, pushing it to the side so I could taste the sweet skin of her neck. A tremor ran through her. I flicked the button open on my jeans and shoved the zipper down. In a flash, I yanked the condom I'd tucked into my pocket out. I paused to glance up.

Olivia stood before me, her spine straight and her head bowed slightly. Her breath came in soft pants and bloody hell it turned me on. I dragged my palm over my cock. I was so hard, all I could think about was being inside of her.

"Bend over," I said, my voice nothing more than a rough whisper.

With the sofa directly in front of her, she didn't hesitate and leaned forward, curling her palms over the back of the sofa.

I shoved my jeans and briefs down just far enough to free my cock and rolled the condom on. I slid a palm down her spine, savoring when she arched, her bottom rising up. I finally gave into what I'd fantasized about so many times since I'd first seen her in her proper little skirt and pushed it up over her hips, almost groaning aloud at the sight of her luscious bottom with a scrap of black silk nestled in the center. I loved her curves and dragged my hands over them, savoring the silk of her skin and the soft give of her flesh. Her breath was coming in heaves, along with mine.

I leaned over and hooked my finger under her thong, pulling it out of the way. She was slicked in wetness, pink and glistening. I couldn't wait anymore and stepped close behind her. Gripping her hips, I positioned my cock at her entrance and sank inside in a swift surge, seating myself deeply. I heard my own groan, a rough broken sound, mingling with hers. Her channel pulsed around me, its warm, silken pressure lashing the whip of lust sharply inside me. With one hand holding tightly to her hip, I slid the other up her spine and threaded my hand in her hair, lightly gripping her curls, as I begun to stroke into her. She arched deeply, her hips pressing back into me with each surge into her. The pressure inside built rapidly, and I felt my release coming. I eased my hand from her hip to reach between her thighs and stroke across her swollen clit. At her cry, I finally let go, my release crashing over me hard and fast.

I curled over her back and slipped my arms around her waist. I wasn't holding onto her for physical support, but it felt as if I was holding on for dear life. This, whatever this madness was with Olivia, made me feel raw and exposed, and only she could ease the fear the feeling elicited.

Several long moments passed before I felt her shiver and realized goose bumps were rising on her skin. I straightened and slowly pulled out of her. She straightened and turned to face me, her skirt still bunched around her hips. "You're cold," I said. Such a mundane comment given the emotions thundering through me, yet it was all I could think to say.

Chapter Twenty

OLIVIA

My car rolled to a stop in my aunt's driveway. I turned the engine off with the click of a button. I loved my little hybrid hatchback and gave the dashboard a pat. I glanced around as I stepped out of the car. The sky was dotted with clouds with the sun peeking out between them. Yellowed birch leaves fell with a gust of wind. Cascade Falls, the small town where I'd grown up, was nestled in the foothills of the Cascade Mountains. It was one of many towns within the broader radius of Seattle, but once you drove off the interstate and into the towering evergreen forests, it was hard to believe Seattle was nearby. After my parents died, my Aunt Lorraine had raised me. She was my mother's fraternal twin sister and so similar to my mother, it was almost strange. Over the years, what I'd called her had morphed affectionately to Lorrie. She was largely responsible for my interest in medicine. She'd been in medical school when my parents died and had dropped out to raise me. She already had her nursing degree at the time and was still working as a nurse in a local pediatrics office to this day. She'd never pressured me, but I shared a natural affinity for every academic subject along the road to medicine, so becoming a doctor had been an easy choice for me.

Her home was a bungalow style, common in the Pacific Northwest, and tucked into the hillside amongst other similar homes. Her beloved garden was fading through the long, slow dance of autumn. I walked down the slate walkway to her front door and stepped inside, calling out as I did.

"Lorrie! It's me."

Her front door opened into a cozy living room with a large stone fireplace to one side and a small dining area to the other. The kitchen was through an alcove behind the dining area. I hung my jacket by the door and walked to the circular dining table, setting down the bag of goodies I'd brought for her. As I was starting a pot of coffee, I heard her footsteps finally and glanced over my shoulder.

"Hey girl," Lorrie said as she reached me and gave me a quick side hug and a peck on the cheek. She turned back to the table and opened the bag. "Oh heaven! You brought hombows and piroshkies."

Lorrie loved Pike's Place Market in downtown Seattle and whenever I went to see her, I made sure to stock up on a few of her favorite baked goods. She loved hombows, which were an Asian stuffed roll, and piroshkies, a Russian baked good, filled with salmon and cream cheese. I'd also brought fresh bread from one of her favorite bakeries.

"There's more. Look in the bottom of the bag. I got some black olive bread and spicy chipotle bread for you." I tapped the start button on the coffee maker and slipped into the chair across from her.

Lorrie's dark curls, so like my mother's and mine, were streaked with silver. She had them tied back in a loose braid. Her brown eyes crinkled at the corners with her smile. "Well, how's life in the big city?"

I shrugged. "Same, same. Busy with work mostly." My reply was what I'd usually say because that was my life for the most part. Except now there was Liam, but I didn't quite know how to talk about him, or how to describe what we were to each other. Just trying made me feel as if I was casting in the dark. I was so unaccustomed to the whims of my emotions tossing me this way and that.

Lorrie absently twirled the end of her braid and eyed me. "Did you happen to see the paper online today?"

Her question threw me. "Huh? No, but I hardly ever do. Why do you ask?"

Lorrie stood and walked over to the coffee table, returning with a newspaper. Sitting down, she flipped through it and spun it around, pointing at a photo. "I doubt anyone else would notice because it's not a good angle, but that sure looks like you."

The photo in question was of me and Liam, taken the night before when we'd been out to dinner. By the grace of dim lighting and no good possibility for a clear view through the restaurant's window, my face was partially in shadow. Liam had been seated facing the window and was easily recognizable. The caption under the photo said: *Who's the mystery woman with Liam Reed, Britain's famous footballer and Seattle's new soccer star?* Of course, this was on the local gossip page of Seattle's biggest newspaper. Under the photo and blurb was a snippet about the betting books in London on Liam and his impossible to guess at love life.

My stomach turned in dread-filled flip and my cheeks flamed scarlet. I knew I couldn't sidestep this with Lorrie, so I gathered myself and looked over at her. "That's me." I put my face in my hands and sighed. "I can't believe this. What if someone else sees that and figures out it's me? I don't know what I was thinking." I lifted my face and swatted a loose curl out of my eyes, my mind spinning. Few people read the physical paper like Lorrie, but everything here would be online with the wonderful comments section in addition. Just thinking about what else might be said made me want to cry. If anyone guessed it was me, I'd be facing plenty of trouble.

Lorrie angled her head to the side, her eyes concerned. "Hon, it's not likely anyone else will be able to tell that's you, except maybe Daisy or Harper. What's got your so worried? I was actually happy to see you finally went on a date. Not because he's some kind of soccer star, but because it'd be nice to see you have a social life."

The coffee maker beeped, and Lorrie quickly stood and stepped to the counter to pour two cups of coffee. I curled my hands around the mug she handed me and took a long swallow, savoring the rich, bitter flavor. "I'm worried because I shouldn't have gone anywhere with him. Technically, he's a former patient, but I operated on him and he's still under the care of the rehab team at the clinic. I'm so stupid," I said with a sigh. Internally, I cringed. Because I had been so ridiculously stupid. I knew better than to cross the lines, but I'd played hopscotch and jumped past every line there was. I was a muddle inside with wishing I'd had the fortitude to steer clear of Liam, the intensity of my feelings for him, the scorching desire between us, and the reality that I needed to take a giant step back and fast before I got in any deeper than I already was.

Lorrie's eyes widened slightly. She was quiet for a moment, taking a sip of her coffee and watching me thoughtfully. "Okay, well, I'm not going to tell you it was the brightest idea. It's a bit of a sticky wicket, but I think you're okay. Even if it wasn't that long ago, he's not your patient now and you didn't have a personal relationship with him before the surgery. Right?"

I nodded, anxiety tightening into a knot in my chest.

Lorrie lifted one shoulder in a slow shrug. "Technically, you're clear. The clinic might think otherwise and there might be clinic policies about this, but don't make trouble where there isn't any yet. It'll probably blow over and nothing will come of it." She paused to take another sip of coffee, her mouth curling in a smile when she set it down. "I gotta say, you're an overachiever at everything. You finally break your years long dating drought with the hottest guy in Seattle. Or at least that's how the gossip pages describe him. What's the status with you two anyway?"

My cheeks were so hot, I needed a fan. Instead, I took a gulp of hot coffee and shrugged. "That's kind of the problem. I don't know what to think. None of this would've happened if Liam hadn't been so damn persistent. I finally caved and went to dinner with him a few weeks back and then again last night. He's completely out of my league, and I have no idea what he sees in me."

Lorrie shook her head sadly. "Hon, you're gorgeous, you just never even let yourself think about much other than academics and now your job. As far as I'm concerned, he's a smart man if he saw past your prickly, cold exterior."

"What do you mean prickly and cold?" I asked, feeling slightly defensive.

"I see how you are. You barely give any man a second glance and you're so focused on work, you let it take over your life. A little scandal wouldn't be a bad thing."

My mouth fell open. "Oh my God. You think a little scandal would be good? You're as bad as Daisy!"

"We both happen to love you to pieces. Ever since your parents died, you've shut down. You used to be a carefree girl. It makes perfect sense that you wouldn't feel so carefree after what happened, but I've hoped for a long time that you might loosen up a bit. Tell me what Liam's like."

I was reeling at her comments, but I wasn't sure how to respond. I could, however, handle telling her about Liam. "He's funny, he's nice... It's weird seeing news stuff about him because I read stuff like that and it's like he's this hotshot sports star. I guess he is, but in person he's just a guy. So there's that and then the mess I've made for myself professionally. I can't believe I let this happen." I adjusted my glasses, anxiety knotting in my chest.

"You like him," Lorrie said softly.

My throat tightened at her words. I was starting to fear my feelings were a lot more than *like*. I took a breath and another gulp of coffee before nodding. "I guess I do. I don't like being in the gossip pages though. It feels like my life was invaded, and no one even knows who I am."

"I doubt anyone likes being in the gossip pages. If they do, they're a reality star and then someday they'll wake up from the nightmare of that," Lorrie said wryly. She reached across the table and squeezed my hand. "Don't worry about that stupid photo. It won't go anywhere. I'd like to meet your Liam."

"He's not *my* Liam." My reply was reflexive, yet I didn't know what to make of Lorrie's quick perception of how much Liam mattered to me.

Lorrie grinned. "Whatever. I'll be in Seattle next month for a nursing conference."

———

I drove back to Seattle late that afternoon, worries about Liam, my poor decision to let myself get involved with him, and that stupid photo lodged firmly in my brain. I'd managed to shove my worries away for the rest of my visit with Lorrie, but alone in the car, it had taken no more than a few minutes for me to turn a photo, which likely no one other than Lorrie had connected to me, into an epic nightmare in my brain. My brain was flipping back and forth between that and wondering when I'd see Liam again.

Waking up beside him was pure heaven. I'd woken to find myself twined against him with my leg tossed over his, my foot tucked between his calves and my body plastered against his side. I tended toward getting cold when I slept, but with Liam as my personal heater, I was warm and toasty. His black locks had been rumpled and his body of all muscle so tempting, I'd nearly climbed atop him. When I'd unconsciously started to explore his muscled chest—because what else was I to do with his delectable body right there?—he'd turned his head to the side, a slow smile curling his lips and his sleepy blue gaze sending a hot shiver through me. One look from him literally curled my toes.

"Good morning, luv," he'd said, his eyes dipping down as he rolled slightly to the side and trailed a hand over the dip of my waist and curve of my hip. He'd proceeded to drive me to near incoherence within minutes. We'd used yet another of the condoms Daisy had generously scattered about my apartment. She'd stopped by a few days after our dinner date and distributed an entire box.

A horn honked from behind me on the interstate, jolting my thoughts off of Liam. I glanced up and realized I was about to drive past my exit. I changed lanes and exited off the highway. Within another few minutes, I reached my apartment door and found it unlocked, immediately figuring Daisy was inside. We had keys to each other's places. I was less likely to stop by hers, solely because I wasn't often in the area unless I was specifically going to see her. Meanwhile, her job and the gym we both used were close to my place. When I opened the door, she was standing at the kitchen counter, twirling her keys on her index finger and talking on the phone.

She waved at me as I slipped out of my shoes and hung up my jacket. She ended her call and plunked down on the couch as I stepped into the kitchen to pour a glass of wine.

"Wine?" I called out.

"Sure. Wanna order takeout?" Before I managed to answer, she continued as if she was conversing with herself. "We should call Harper and tell her to come by. We haven't had a girls' night-in in forever. She called and said she'd be over this way for some meeting this afternoon."

I carried our two glasses of wine over to the couch, handing one to Daisy and sitting down. "Girls' night-in sounds good to me." We'd coined that term during college when we needed to study and wanted company. The three of us would spread dinner out on whatever empty surfaces were available and study into the wee hours of the morning. We didn't need to study anymore, but we still tried to get together like that every so often. I'd been resisting the urge to see Liam and could seriously use some advice, so it was perfect. "I'll call Harper, you order takeout."

Daisy took a swallow of her wine and twirled the glass slowly in her hand. "Anything you want?"

"You pick."

"Okay, then it's pizza. It's shark week for me, so I need carbs and cheese."

'Shark week' was shorthand for that time of the month. We'd simultaneously come up with the nickname one summer when we were deep into studying for board exams and the nature channel's week long special on sharks happened to be on.

I slipped my phone out of my pocket to call Harper. "Pizza works for me. I don't need an excuse."

Hours later, the three of us were lounging on the couch in half comas from the food and wine. I'd yet to bring up the photo in the paper and likely all over the place online because I didn't like thinking about it. They'd teased me about Liam, but otherwise Harper had a mini family crisis with her mother in the midst of chemo for breast cancer and in a rough patch, so our conversation had been focused else-where. We'd moved onto lighter topics, and I was relaxed enough that I finally got up the nerve to say something.

"Did either one of you see the paper or the news online today?" I asked.

Harper rolled her head to the side on the back of the couch, her eyes curious. "You mean the Seattle Observer?"

I nodded as she shook her head. "No. Any reason you're asking?"

Daisy glanced to me as well, arching a brow. "Is this a current events quiz?"

I rolled my eyes. "God no. Anyway, I went out to see Lorrie today and there's a photo of me with Liam in there. You can't really tell it's me, but I don't know what the hell to do."

Harper straightened and Daisy sat up with a squeal. "Oh this is awesome! You and Liam are news."

"How is this awesome? I'm not news yet because you can barely see me, and I'd rather it stays that way. My God, it's not the best move for me to even be with him, much less end up in the gossip pages."

Daisy waved a hand dismissively. "If you're going to be so freaked out over your job, you should just go tell Dr. Adams you went out to dinner with Liam. She'll give you some crap about it and then you can stop worrying. They won't fire you. It'd be one thing if Liam filed a complaint, but it's not like that's happening. No way. You're the best surgeon they have, and you've had too many high-profile cases with glowing recommendations. I know you don't like thinking about it this way, but you're a moneymaker for them."

Harper nodded along with Daisy's words. I looked between them. "You really think I should tell her?"

Dr. Helen Adams was my direct supervisor at the clinic. She'd recruited me straight out of med school. I respected her immensely and felt lucky to have a boss I actually liked as well. She'd stopped doing surgeries a year ago after she developed arthritis in one of her hands. She consulted on cases all over the world. As crazy as part of me thought Daisy's idea was, it might keep me from driving myself mad with worry over the whole thing. I had enough to juggle in my brain—and heart—when it came to Liam.

Harper spoke up. "I do. You're going to drive yourself nuts if you don't. You can't really undo the fact you've had dinner with him twice and..."

"Screwed his brains out," Daisy interjected with a grin.

Harper rolled her eyes and continued. "You're going to be all paranoid about it even if you don't keep seeing him. If you do keep seeing him, there will definitely be more photos like that. He's a public figure whether you like it or not. If you talk to Dr. Adams now, you can head off the whole mess becoming a scandal."

I leaned back into the couch again and looked between them. "Huh? Well, maybe I will. I'll think about it."

"In the meantime, bets on how long it takes the rumor mill to name you?" Daisy asked with a sly grin.

"It's not funny! I don't like this. I still can't figure out how I ended up here. We don't exactly have anything in common, and I don't know..."

A balled up napkin bounced off my head. "Stop it! You're just putting up barriers. If you ask me, you're scared because someone got under your iron skin," Daisy declared.

Harper laughed softly. "Okay, a bit harsh, but kinda true."

"Fine. Either way, he's a world-famous sports star and I'm a doctor. I mean, they have official bets on when he'll get hitched to someone. That's is so *not* the kind of guy I should throw my career on the line for. It's insane," I said.

Daisy shrugged. "He's just a guy. 'Should' doesn't really matter, and it's silly anyway to say who should fall for who. Maybe he is famous, and obviously he's hella good at soccer, but I liked him when I met him. He's funny and nice and pretty damn normal." She glanced to Harper. "You should meet him. You're our barometer."

This time Harper rolled her eyes. "That's silly. I'd like to meet him though. Any guy that's got you all in a dither is worth meeting."

"I'm in a dither?"

Daisy and Harper's gazes swung to me in unison. "Uh, yeah. Your eyes go all dreamy half the time now," Daisy said with a choked laugh.

My cheeks got hot, and I took a gulp of wine. *Dreamy.* As much as I wanted to argue the point, I knew it to be true, and it terrified me.

Chapter Twenty-One

LIAM

I walked down the hall at the stadium, heading to Coach's office for a meeting. I figured he wanted to check in about my status. I knew he spoke regularly with Tim and Dr. Monroe. As far as I was concerned, if he wanted to put me on the field sooner than the agreed upon full three months since my surgery, I was ready. It was over a month and a half since Olivia worked her magic on my knee, and I felt good. When I did my PT, there was no lingering pain. The only time I noticed anything was when I first woke up. It was like I needed a bit of grease to oil the joint, and a hot shower did the trick. I'd tried to cajole Tim into bumping up the time-frame, but he was a stubborn bloke, or so I was learning. He insisted my knee needed to be ready for the potential for abrupt motion and was starting on me on a new series of exercises to simulate what my knee would go through during play.

My footsteps were the only sound as I walked along the concrete floors. I loved being in stadiums when they were mostly empty. The spaces felt like hallowed ground then, when the crescendo of the crowds was nothing more than a distant echo, but the feeling I got from playing beat like a drum inside me in the quiet. Coach's door was open, but I paused beside it and rapped my knuckles. He looked up from his computer and waved me in.

"Come on in, Liam. Have a seat," he said, gesturing to the chair on the opposite side of his desk.

I sat down and leaned back in my chair. Coach angled his head to the side, his perceptive gaze holding mine. After a moment of quiet, he spoke. "I hear from Tim that you might be ahead of schedule with your recovery. He tells me you're pushing him to clear you to return sooner."

I nodded. "I feel good. Can't help but try, eh?"

Coach grinned. "Perhaps not, but you're waiting. I'd rather have you in tip-top shape than back a little early. Anything else isn't worth the risk. I appreciate how much work you've put into your recovery and also the help you offered Matt. He's not you and never will be, but whatever you said to him before our game the night before last helped."

After watching a few challenging practices, I'd taken Matt aside and given him some feedback on how to navigate with the team. Being the playmaker was more than raw physical skill. It involved a deep, tactical understanding of how your particular team meshed. Alex had also gone out of his way to ease the pressure on Matt. I took a breath and nodded. "I'd like to take full credit, but Alex has done his part too. Matt's under gobs of pressure. He's holding up well, all in all."

Coach nodded and picked up a slinky on his desk, idly stretching it back and forth in his hands. He was quiet again for a few beats and I wondered just what he wanted to meet with me about. "I'm sure you're accustomed to it, but you were in the news last weekend. It doesn't appear that kind of gossip interfered with your playing back in Britain, so I hope it doesn't here."

I was flummoxed and had no clue what Coach was referencing. "Come again?"

He tugged his laptop towards him on the desk. Pulling up his computer screen, he clicked through it and then spun it around, tapping his finger on a picture. I leaned forward to see a photo of Olivia and me from our dinner last weekend. I happened to be facing the window, so it was easy to tell who I was. Olivia was angled away with her face in shadow. A bolt of anger shot through me. I'd learned to ignore this bullshit, but it wasn't fair to Olivia and I knew she was probably freaking out.

"Bloody hell," I said, leaning back and running a hand through my hair. I'd never enjoyed the nosiness of the media and certainly didn't want Olivia to get nervous over this.

"Anyone special?" Coach asked, only his eyes giving away the hint of a smile.

Only the most special woman I'd ever met. But I wasn't about to say that aloud. Olivia had been politely sidestepping me when I tried to see her again. It had been four days since waking up beside her last Sunday, and I was about out of my mind with missing her. The usual me would've already moved on, but the usual me rarely actually slept with a woman. There was sex, but I typically made my way to my own bed. I could only wonder if she'd seen the photo online.

My face must've given something away because Coach nodded slowly. "So she is someone special. Well, from my experience, that's a good thing."

I couldn't help but be curious about what he meant. I wasn't accustomed to being tied up in knots inside. Especially over a woman. "What do you mean?"

Coach gave me a considering gaze and then shrugged. "The life that comes with playing soccer internationally, or any sport for that matter, isn't easy. It's wearing and the fawning attention from the media is nothing more than an annoying distraction. Actually finding someone you care about is a good thing no matter what, but in this life, it gives you something you don't have otherwise—a center for your life and something more important. A woman you love becomes the biggest play of your life, no game will ever come close."

I stared maybe a few beats too long, my heart banging hard and fast against my ribs. I didn't quite know what to think. I wasn't so stupid as to pretend Olivia wasn't special, but *love?* I swallowed against the emotion tightening my chest and throat. When I didn't say anything, Coach continued. "Also, you don't strike me as the kind of guy who'd fly solo forever. You come from a close family, and you have a good head on your shoulders. No need to fill me in, but if she's special, don't be stupid and let her get away."

He winked and spun in his chair when his desk phone rang. "Hang on," he said, quickly picking up the phone. He nodded at whatever the other person said and then glanced to me, covering the phone with his hand. "I need to take this. Unless you'd like to talk more, we're done. Stick to the PT plan you have and no pushing too hard. Got that?"

I nodded and stood. "Mind closing the door for me, Liam?" he called out as I walked through it. I gave a thumbs up, closed the door behind me and walked down the hall in a semi-daze. I was mentally spinning in circles. I don't know why what Coach said knocked me sideways, but it did. I supposed it was that even though I had enough sense to realize the way I felt about Olivia was like nothing I'd felt before, I hadn't had anyone ask me aloud what she meant to me. I needed to see her. Now.

Chapter Twenty-Two

OLIVIA

I brushed my hands over the thin fabric of my scrubs, which did hardly anything to help with the nervous sweat on my palms. I'd performed two surgeries this morning, both of which had gone well. This afternoon was my usual meeting time with Dr. Adams, and I'd spent every day this week worrying about whether or not to talk to her about my dinners with Liam. I'd even called Harper again last night to ruminate aloud. Since Daisy tended toward more emotionally driven advice, I often turned to Harper, who was ever rational, for a reality check. Harper was firmly in the camp that I should talk with Dr. Adams.

"Either that, or you do what you're doing now, which is driving yourself crazy worrying. The other thing is it seems like Liam actually means something to you. If that's the case, you don't want to put yourself in a spot where things get messier than they need to be," Harper had said softly.

I hadn't been able to bring myself to admit Liam was starting to mean *way* too much. I hadn't been out and out avoiding him, but I'd had excuses not to see him ever since he'd left my apartment Sunday morning. They were legitimate excuses and all related to work, but I could find those anytime between meetings, after hours consultation and the charting documentation that never ended. I was unsettled and out of sorts over the stupid photo.

I'd scrabbled together my nerve and sat across the desk from Dr. Adams while she finished a phone call. When she set the phone down, she adjusted her glasses and smiled over at me. "Sorry about that. How are you today, Olivia?"

I swallowed and managed a nervous smile. "Okay. It's been a busy week for surgeries, but all have gone well."

She smoothed a hand over her short gray hair and nodded, her bright blue eyes warm. "Of course they went well! You're an excellent surgeon. Let's take a look at some numbers."

She started to turn in her chair. I knew she likely wanted to review our unit's quarterly stats on patients seen, recovery times and the like, but I knew once we got started, the only hour I had with her this week would be gone. I was so tempted to nod and go along, but I'd gotten myself so ready to get this over with, I had to. "Actually, there was something I was hoping to discuss before we got to that."

She spun her chair to face me again, her eyebrows lifting in question. She was a slender woman, her features sharp and defined, softened only by the kindness in her eyes. I hoped I could count on her kindness to get me through this.

I took a deep breath, adjusted my glasses and forced myself to speak. "I can't quite believe I'm about to say this, but I had dinner twice with a patient I operated on last month. I know it shouldn't have happened, and I don't have any good reason other than he kept asking me. I decided I should come talk to you about it because I don't want to cause problems, and I'm worried it will. If I'm in trouble, please just tell me now." My words tumbled out in a rush, and I only stopped when I ran out of breath.

I adjusted my glasses again and then twisted my hands together in my lap. I had to force myself to look back at her. Dr. Adams' expression had gone flat—which I knew to mean she was thinking something, but she was trying to keep it from showing. My stomach was churning so hard, I prayed I wouldn't actually vomit. I couldn't believe how stupid I'd been. All my life, I'd been one of the 'good girls.' I never got in trouble at school, I never had a grade lower than an A, and I followed the rules everywhere I went. I was that person who actually came to a full stop at stop signs in the middle of nowhere. Which is why I couldn't quite believe how much I'd lost my mind over Liam. Until I'd seen that damn photo, I'd been stumbling about in a daze. Oh, I'd been worried about the boundaries I was crossing, but to say I'd been in a bit of a haze of lust was an understatement. The photo had been like ice water dumped on my head.

Dr. Adams' expression shifted from flat to bemused. She leaned back in her chair and drummed her fingers on the desk. "Let me guess. Liam Reed?"

My cheeks got hot instantly. I swallowed and nodded. "How...?"

"I happened to see him in the gym with Tim the other day. You were on your way out and his eyes were glued to you." She took a breath, her gaze sobering again. "I obviously don't need to tell you this was definitely not a good choice."

My gut kept churning away, and I swallowed. Oh, I knew perfectly well what I'd done was not a good choice. That was putting it mildly.

"I know. I don't know what I was thinking. I won't see him again and if I'm fired, just tell me now."

Dr. Adams sighed. "Olivia, I'm not firing you. The ethics on this aren't as black and white as you might think. There is a suggested guideline that doctors shouldn't pursue a romantic relationship until more than six months have passed since they treated a patient. Obviously, it's only been about six weeks, and Liam is still a patient with the clinic. I know he's formally discharged from surgical care, but we're on shaky ground if we pretend like you have nothing to do with his care. If he experiences any complications, you would be the consulting physician. That's not an option now. I'll need to set it up in the system so you have no access to his health records, and I'll need to talk with Tim to make sure he doesn't seek you out for additional consultation. If Liam has any future need for follow up, you cannot treat him. I know you're not going to like it, but I will notify the clinic board. They may decide to formally reprimand you, and I obviously have to write you up. The worst case here would be a formal reprimand, but the clinic will only want to do damage control. Liam is a consenting adult and clearly pursued you. If it were any other scenario, it wouldn't matter how valuable you are to the clinic. If you're worried about your medical license, the only worry you have there is if Liam decides to file a complaint. I'm guessing that won't be a problem. As for your employment status, I'm shocked, but it doesn't change the fact I trust you completely as a doctor and don't doubt your ability to provide excellent care. It speaks highly of you that you came to me. I'd rather find out from you than another way."

My heart was still racing and my stomach churning madly, but I managed to take a deep breath and nod. Relief washed through me. Not because she didn't fire me, but because I'd finally gotten it off my chest. I'd have to face the music with the clinic board, but I could handle that. I twisted my hands and wiped them on my scrubs again. I wasn't sure what else to say. It had taken all of my where-withal to get through the last bit, and I didn't have it in me to think much more.

Dr. Adams saved me by shifting focus slightly. "Forgive me if I'm being too personal here, but it's so unlike you to do something like this, I can't help but wonder what Liam means to you."

My heart set off on another gallop. Liam meant way too much to me, and I had no idea what to do about any of it. I looked over at Dr. Adams and almost burst into tears. Her perceptive gaze met mine, and she sighed softly. "Oh, I see. Well, if you're going to set yourself up for an HR write up and a board reprimand, it might as well be for someone who matters." My mouth fell open, but I snapped it shut. I didn't know what to think of everyone around me so easily honing in on how much Liam had gotten to me. For a moment, I thought she might say more, but she didn't. After a few beats of quiet, she spun in her chair. "Let's look at those numbers."

———

A few hours later, I walked home through the light rain. It was chilly, and I'd forgotten my raincoat at the clinic. I started shivering as soon as my thin cotton scrubs got wet, but I doggedly kept walking, figuring it was only a fifteen-minute walk. After my meeting with Dr. Adams, the rest of the day had gone by in a blur. I was beyond relieved I'd finally talked with her. Yet, my brain had promptly shifted gears to worrying about what to do about my feelings for Liam. He wasn't just some guy. I was terrified I might be falling in love with him and guessed that was the furthest thing from his mind. The usual me would want to box myself away from him, but oddly I wanted to see him, as if he could somehow make me feel better. How I'd been so stupid to fall for an internationally famous footballer with women all over the world lusting after him, I didn't know. I had enough sense to know he'd likely pursued me because I tried to turn him down. Once the novelty of that wore off, his attention would drift elsewhere.

I was looking down at the sidewalk as I walked up to my building, idly counting the cracks as I stepped over them. I fumbled for my keys, but my hands were cold and my keys fell in a clatter to the ground. I leaned over to pick them up, but not before a man's hand curled over them, a hand I recognized the second I saw it. Liam had sexy hands, hands that sent shivers through me in more ways than one—strong, nimble and slightly battered with a few scars. My breath caught, and I whipped my head up, straightening to find Liam standing beside the door. I'd been so out of it, I hadn't even noticed him. His black hair was damp, his blue eyes bright in the rainy gray light. His mouth curled at one corner. "Hello luv. You're all wet."

I ran a hand over my damp hair. Curls were escaping willy-nilly. I felt about as attractive as a lump of mud in my scrubs after a long day at work, an emotionally draining meeting with my boss, and my mind stuck on the hamster wheel of Liam. Yet, I was so happy to see him, I smiled. His return grin was wide and like the sun coming out after days of rain. "You shan't chase me off just yet. I decided since you kept coming up with your reasons for being too busy, I'd drop by your flat. Shall we go up then?"

I didn't even hesitate and nodded. When I tried to fit the key in the door, my hands were cold enough, they weren't working too well. Liam stepped beside me and curled his warm hand over mine. "Let me get it."

Shivering in the wet cold, I nodded and handed him the keys. He had us through the door quickly and placed a warm palm on my back as we walked up the stairs. He didn't say anything, and I didn't know what to say. The day had been so full of stressful and confusing feelings, I wanted nothing more than to get warm and dry and curl up beside him.

Once we were in my apartment, I looked toward him. His eyes coasted over me. "You're shivering. Shower for you," he said matter-of-factly.

Next thing I knew, he'd peeled me out of my scrubs and started the shower. There was nothing sexual about his touch, and it was strangely comforting. He chucked his own clothes off at the last minute and followed me into the shower. With the steaming water running over me, I finally started to thaw. We traded the soap, and I turned to face him. All of the sudden, tears welled and a sob broke from me.

Chapter Twenty-Three

LIAM

Olivia's looked over at me, her dark lashes spiky and her green eyes luminous in the steam. The moment I'd seen her walking toward her building, I'd known something was off. Her shoulders had been hunched against the rain, her eyes weary when she'd first seen me, exuding a sense of vulnerability. Just now, pain and confusion flashed in her eyes. The soap slipped from her hands, falling to the shower floor with a thump, and she burst into tears, burying her face in her hands.

I didn't even stop to think. All I knew was I would do anything to erase her pain. I wrapped her in my arms, sliding my hand up and down her back in slow passes and murmuring against her hair. Water sluiced over us and steam billowed around us as I held her. She slowly lowered her hands, relaxing in my hold and slipping her arms around my waist. She trembled slightly, but her sobs slowed by degrees, and I finally felt her take a deep breath. She'd buried her face in my chest and slowly lifted it. I loosened my hold and leaned back enough to look down at her. A bolt of pain slashed me—her pain was my pain. I didn't have to know what it was about. Her eyes held mine in the misty air.

My chest felt tight, and my heart started to pound hard and fast. Olivia slid her hands around my waist, sliding across my slippery skin and up my chest. The air around us felt electrified. Whatever she'd been feeling appeared to have eased. Her gaze locked with mine, dark and intent. I was becoming accustomed to my inability to control anything that happened with her. Just now, part of me held onto the worry about what had caused her to burst into tears. Me, the man who'd never wanted a woman to read too much into anything, was worrying Olivia would think it was all about sex.

My body, on the other hand, thought it was bloody perfect to have Olivia's hands exploring me. Her touch became rushed and frantic, almost as if she wanted to lose herself. I reached for her, but she dodged, her lips following her hands. My breath came out in a hiss when she placed a palm on my chest and firmly pushed me. My back collided with the cool tile wall as she shimmied down and curled her hand around my cock, which had gone rock hard in a matter of seconds the moment the energy between us shifted.

She glanced up through her wet lashes, her eyes locking to mine, as she leaned forward and dragged her tongue along the underside of my cock. My head fell to the tile wall with a thunk as her mouth closed over me, and she set to drive me completely mindless.

If there was one thing I'd come to learn about Olivia was she approached things thoroughly. I had enough sense to know she hadn't become so well-known as a surgeon by chance. No, I was certain she'd been a straight A-plus student, which naturally lent itself to the understanding she was a woman of focus and intent. Just now, that focus and intent was pointed like a laser at me. Or more specifically, my cock. And holy hell was that the best thing ever. In the entire universe. Her warm, wet mouth took me in again and again with her tongue driving me mad in between with long, slow strokes. I was close, so close to release, but I needed to be inside of her.

I reached for her, pulling her up more roughly than I intended, but I was so far gone, all I could think about was getting as close as possible to her. I lifted her against me. She gratified me by instantly winding her legs around me. I could feel the slick heat of her against me and gritted my teeth. I hadn't thought far enough ahead to cart condoms into the shower.

"Olivia. Wait," I bit out when she tightened her legs around my hips and arched against me.

She lightly bit my neck and mumbled something. I pushed the glass door open with my shoulder, juggling her against me.

"Where are you going?" she asked, leaning back to look at me.

I was in almost physical pain from holding back, but I managed to speak. "Condom."

Her eyes widened, a smile spreading. "Right there," she said, pointing to a basket hanging from the showerhead. Shampoo and other assorted bath products were overflowing, but I certainly didn't see any condoms. She reached over my shoulder and shoved the shampoo out of the way, coming up with a condom. In seconds, she tore the packet open, and I positioned my cock at her entrance. I forced myself to wait because I needed to see her.

I brushed a wet curl out of her eyes. "Olivia."

Her eyes lifted to meet mine, and she curled her legs more tightly around me. Our gazes stayed locked together as I sank slowly inside her. Her eyes widened when I seated myself fully within her creamy clench. A wave of emotion crested within me, and I pulled her closer until our bodies were plastered together. Our skin was slick from the hot water raining down over us. Her nipples were taut and felt so damn good against my chest, I almost came without even moving. But I needed to move, needed to feel her release. With the wall behind me and her twined around me, I couldn't move much, but I didn't need to. We rocked slowly together. Her channel throbbed as soft pants and cries came from her. Lust was coiled so tightly inside me, the pressure built and built until she arched against me and cried out. My release followed hers with a raw shout as her channel tightened and pulsed around me.

Her head fell against my shoulder. I held her close and closed my eyes, savoring the feel of her surrounding me. After several long moments, we untangled ourselves, climbed out of the shower and dried off. Whatever had been weighing on Olivia earlier seemed to have dissipated. She dressed in soft fleece pants and a top, made hot chocolate and nudged me into bed with her, all of which I was perfectly happy to go along with.

"On my way home, all I wanted was to get warm and dry." She paused and bit her lip, her cheeks flushing slightly. I loved it. "I got more than I bargained for, but I still want warm, so we're watching TV in here."

She dragged extra pillows into her bedroom from the couch and piled them high. I lay in bed later, listening to Olivia's steady breathing as she slept beside me. She was definitely warm and dry, and my heart was tripping uncertainly along this road I'd never taken. I was still wondering what had put the pain in Olivia's eyes earlier, but hadn't wanted to push. There was also the rather inconvenient fact I had next to no clue how to navigate this emotional terrain. It wasn't something I'd dealt with before and it set me back on my heels. I liked to feel in control and most of my life I did. Being a world-class athlete, no matter the sport in question, meant a level of commitment, concentration and discipline, all of which signified control on a meta level. I was entirely comfortable feeling as if I was master of the play on the pitch, which dominated my life.

Whatever this was with Olivia had shaken me because I

felt out of control, tumbling along in forces of desire and emotion. The last few months of my life in general had shaken me, what with my mother's sudden death, being signed to a new team in another country, and being sidelined by my knee injury. Of all of those events, my mother's death and my feelings for Olivia shared the most because they involved my heart. The trade and my knee were things I could manage. My emotions, well they were something else altogether.

When Olivia shifted onto her side, her lush bottom bumping against my hip, I rolled to face her and pulled her close against me, nuzzling into the soft curve of her neck. I fell asleep breathing in the scent of her.

Chapter Twenty-Four

OLIVIA

At the sound of a knock on my office door, I called out for whomever it was to come in. Tim Maxwell stepped inside, closing the door behind him. Tim was one of our best physical therapists and rehab coaches. We had plenty of PT's on staff with incredible skill, yet Tim's way of approaching clients took his care to the next level. He wasn't intimidated by pro athletes and had absolutely no problem standing up to them if they tried to push their recovery too fast. He was also one of the nicest guys I knew and a friend. I wouldn't usually feel the slightest bit of anxiety about seeing him, yet I knew it was likely Dr. Adams had pulled him aside to inform him he couldn't consult with me about Liam.

"Hey Tim. How's it going?" I asked, striving to keep my anxiety from bubbling up too much.

He sat down across from my desk and eyed me for a long moment, which served only to spin the anxiety faster inside. "So, I understand I'm not to consult with you if any complications arise with Liam Reed's recovery."

I adjusted my glasses and nodded. My relief at talking to Dr. Adams didn't keep me from beating myself up for even being in this mess to begin with. I'd promised myself I'd find a way to end whatever it was I was doing with Liam, and instead I'd spent another night with him. I swatted those thoughts away and focused on the moment. Marshaling, my composure, I met Tim's gaze. "That's right."

A slow smile spread across Tim's face. "I never thought you'd be the one in this situation. How'd Dr. Adams handle it when you talked with her?"

"As well as could be expected. I'm just praying whatever the clinic board does isn't too awful," I said with a sigh.

Tim's smile faded. "They'll do something, but you won't lose your position here. You're too valuable, and you did the right thing by going to Dr. Adams." He paused, his gaze considering. "You surprised me, but it didn't surprise me a bit the man in question happened to be Liam. That man can hardly keep his eyes off of you. I must admit I warned him off. Liam's a nice guy, but I'd hate to see you get hurt. I don't think he'd mean to hurt you, but he's one of Britain's favorite heartthrobs and on his way to that here in Seattle. Don't suppose you'd tell me if this is serious?"

Tim's comments struck right at the heart of my insecurities and my fears about how far and fast I'd fallen for Liam. I closed my eyes and took a breath before meeting his gaze again. His warm brown eyes eased my anxiety slightly. "I don't know what to think. You're as surprised as me that I'm in this situation. Liam...well, he's a bit difficult to resist..."

"And he *really* likes you if the way he looks at you means anything," Tim interjected.

I flushed and continued. "I don't know what to think. It's not like we have much in common, but when I'm with him, I don't think about the fact he's an international soccer star with half the women in the world drooling over him. I have no idea what I'm doing or where this is going." I swallowed and fought back a rush of emotion, remembering the other night when I'd fallen apart in the shower. Liam hadn't hesitated and wrapped me in his strong, solid embrace, nothing other than the feel of being held by him helping to ease the confusion and fear tumbling through me. Falling asleep with him curled around me was the best thing. Ever. Well, that and waking up with him. Better yet, having him inside me with the wild gallop of longing finally sated and an intimacy so intense binding us together, I could hardly stand to think of it.

Tim looked over at me, his eyes conveying warmth and understanding. "Oh hon, I think you might be in love," he said softly.

My breath caught and I almost cried, shaking my head vehemently. "No, no, I can't be. This is just lust and I'm not used to it. It'll pass. Aside from all that, I need to clean up the mess I've made by even getting involved with him. It won't do for me to keep this going."

Tim arched a brow and eyed me for a long moment. "Okay, two things. First, I like Liam. He's a good guy. It's obvious his family means a lot to him, which is a good thing. He doesn't talk about it much, but I can tell his mother's death has been hard on him. In no way am I saying that's good, just that it tells you something about his character. Maybe you should stop worrying about how you're different. Second, you've already cleaned up the mess. You told Dr. Adams. She's completely removed you from any possibility of being involved in follow up consultations. Sure, you have to deal with the board thing, but you have to do that anyway. Don't shut yourself off from something just because you have an easy out."

Tim's pointed words struck at me. I didn't like to think I was looking for excuses, but perhaps I was. It didn't change the reality that I felt I was in way over my head. "No matter what, I don't even know what Liam wants, and to say our lives are worlds apart is a bit of an understatement. I do surgery, and he plays ball. I mind my own business, and he gets reported on in gossip news."

Tim shrugged. "Don't even go there in your head. Focus

on what's happening, instead of all the reasons you're differ-ent. Look around you. Most people that are together aren't together because they're so alike. Right now, Liam is into you. Trust me, I see the way he looks at you. You're obvi-ously *way* into him, or you wouldn't even be talking to me about this. I might've been surprised, but I'm happy to see you focus on something other than work." His pager beeped. Tim stood and gave me a hard look. "Do me a favor and don't let your head get in the way."

At that, he strode out of the office. I spun in my chair and stared out the windows. The sky was partially clear this morning. Puget Sound glittered under shafts of sun falling through the clouds. I'd felt a sense of relief coming to work this week, finally free of the burden of worrying about hiding what was happening with Liam. Yet, I couldn't shake the disquiet over my feelings for Liam. With a shake of my head, I batted the thoughts away.

A few hours later I was still at work when my phone vibrated with a text from Daisy. *I'll kill him for you.*

Completely puzzled, I texted back. *What?*

Online Seattle Observer.

I clicked out of our records system and online, quickly looking up the Seattle Observer. Right there on the main page was a photo of Liam seated on a bench outside of the Seattle Stars stadium. It wasn't just a photo of Liam, but of a woman practically in his lap. If she wasn't actually a model, she should've been. She was willowy with glossy blonde hair. She was leaning forward, her cleavage displayed perfectly for his view. I felt sick—sick with a flash of jealousy and sick to find myself questioning him. I hated it, but I couldn't help myself from clicking on the photo that led to a brief article that offered me nothing except more anxiety and the clear understanding I was most definitely in over my head.

Liam Reed, one of Britain's favorite footballers, with Millie Morton, the one and only woman believed to come close to stealing his heart. Ms. Morton remains a favorite on the runway and will be on hand for the Seattle Stars exhibition match in a few months. She made a surprise appearance in Seattle a bit sooner than expected. While the match is for show only, Mr. Reed is expected to be back in play by then. We're all looking forward to the potential fireworks. Meanwhile, there have been no further sightings of the mystery woman seen with Mr. Reed here in Seattle.

Everything I'd just said to Tim came slamming to the fore. My life was so very different from Liam's. I needed to get my mind back onto my career, not be wondering what I might mean to Liam, while he was flirting with a woman who'd apparently seen fit to fly to Seattle to visit him. This photo was representative of every reason why I needed to take my heart out of this game with Liam. I sat right where I was, unmoving for several long minutes, before texting Daisy again. *No need to kill him. A wake up call for me.*

I set my phone down and swallowed against the tightness in my throat and the tears pressing hot at the back of my eyes. After a few shaky breaths, I nodded to myself. This was the best thing. I needed something to push me to stop being so foolish.

Chapter Twenty-Five

LIAM

I drained the bottle of water Tim handed me and set it down on the floor before glancing to him. "Well?" I asked.

Tim stood with a hand on one hip, his breath coming in steady heaves as mine was. We'd just finished a forty-five minute run on the treadmill with Tim putting me through a grueling interval workout with simulated hills and abrupt jolts to force me to brace my knee. Despite the fact all of it happened on a machine, it felt damn close to what I'd be doing in active play. Tim nodded slowly. "You're looking good. I have to say, I'm pretty tempted to clear you a week sooner, but I don't think Coach Hoffman will go for it."

I grinned, a massive sense of relief following immediately. "You don't say? Well, I'll bloody fight ol' Bernie on this."

Tim returned my grin and shook his head slowly. "Don't think you'll win that one." He sobered. "Honestly, Coach Hoffman takes good care of his players. I'm more used to coaches who want to rush recoveries. Hoffman would prefer you back without having to turn around and send you right back to me. I'll let him know I think you're ready, but you're welcome to keep working out with me until the initial deadline we selected."

I leaned against the wall and crossed my arms over my chest. "Right. I'd be shocked if Coach let me start sooner." With a shrug, I pushed off the wall. "You'll be seeing me then."

I started to head toward the shower when Tim said my name. Turning back, I arched a brow. "Yes?"

Tim and I happened to be alone in the gym, but nevertheless, he walked to me. "Olivia," was all he said.

The moment he said her name, my heart gave a resounding thump. Olivia. Not more than a few minutes passed in any given day that I wasn't thinking about her. Ever since last weekend, she'd been dodging me again, which bothered me far more than I'd like to admit. After our last night together, I'd started to face what she meant to me. Although it unsettled me, I could hardly tolerate the idea of her not being a part of my life.

I realized Tim was waiting. "What about Olivia?"

"I'm going to guess you'd already ignored my request to steer clear of her before I mentioned it."

I held his gaze and nodded slowly. I respected Tim and had enough sense to know he was only out to take care of Olivia. If I hadn't already known he was in a committed relationship with a man, I might've experienced a flash of jealousy—a feeling I'd most certainly never experienced.

Tim looked as if he was considering his words carefully. He crossed his arms and tilted his head down, the warning in his gaze clear. "I'm not sure if she told you, but she let her director know what was going on. As a result, she's under orders not to consult on your case if needed. She's an adult, so she's obviously responsible for her own choices, but you have to understand this isn't the kind of thing Olivia does. She's not what I'd call experienced with relationships and certainly not with men like you. I respect you. I honestly think you're a decent guy, but you'd best not hurt her. There aren't many people like her in the world—she's nothing other than honest and good-hearted and one of the most brilliant people I know."

My chest tightened and my pulse kicked up a notch. Olivia hadn't mentioned she'd told her director about us. I wondered what that meant. I knew everything Tim said about her and the person she was to be true. I knew on the outside it might seem as if I was after Olivia if only because she was a novelty to me. Perhaps that had been the case at first, but even then it didn't feel right to consider it that way. All I knew was I'd taken one look at her and wanted her down to my bones. The more I learned about her, the closer I felt. She'd snuck into my heart without even trying. I knew she might wonder what I saw in her, but that's only because she was the opposite of vain. She was flat beautiful and didn't even know it. I loved that there was never a moment where I wondered if she was spending time with me solely because of who I was. If anything, my career and public role were a mark against me in her eyes.

I looked to Tim again and cleared my throat. "Olivia means a lot to me," I finally said.

He nodded. "Right then. Take good care of her."

At that, he turned away, heading back toward where his office was. I remained still for a few beats before heading for the shower. I needed to see Olivia.

Luck was with me when I arrived at Olivia's building, and another resident leaving held the door for me. I slipped in and swiftly climbed the stairs to her flat. It was past two months since I'd torn my meniscus. It felt like a distant memory now. I could climb the stairs with ease, and I knew it was due to Tim's rigorous and careful rehab plan. Had it been left to me, I most definitely would've pushed myself too far and too fast. I cleared the last stair on the third floor and aimed straight for Olivia's door. It was close to dark outside, and I hoped to find her home. Knowing she'd spoken with her director about us, I hadn't wanted to seek her out at the clinic. After knocking several times with nothing but silence echoing back to me, I leaned against the wall with a sigh.

To hell with worrying about her director, I'd hunt her down at work if I had to. Once I was out of her building, I covered the blocks from her flat to the clinic inside of five minutes. The clinic doors were open, but the place was quiet, much of the bustle of the day gone. A few people were in the main waiting area. I walked past and turned down the hallway leading toward Olivia's office. I could see as I approached that her door was open. A sense of euphoria started to rise within. That's all it took—the simple knowledge I might be about to see her lifted me up inside.

I didn't even pause and turned into her office. She stood by the windows, her arms crossed. It didn't appear she'd heard me. I walked straight to her and slid my hands down her arms, leaning to drop a kiss on the back of her neck and breathe in her scent. "Hello, luv," I mumbled against her skin, gratified at the goose bumps that rose under my lips.

For a moment, she started to lean back into me, her body softening, but then she stiffened and stepped away. Confused, I lifted my head to find her taking enough steps away that it was obvious she wanted distance between us. I stared at her, trying to read her. Her expression was tight, her eyes anxious.

"Liam, we can't keep doing this."

My heart started pounding so hard it hurt. Meanwhile, my stomach knotted because I didn't like the look in her eyes—anxious and closed. She crossed her arms more tightly as if shielding herself from me.

"What do you mean?" I asked, taking a step to close the chasm she'd created between us. I didn't push too far because I wanted her to have the space she seemed to need.

She waved a hand back and forth between us. "This! Us! I told my director because I don't like keeping secrets. I don't do this kind of thing! I just don't. I have to wait and see if the clinic board will reprimand me. And then there's you. I'm not stupid. I know I'm not the kind of woman you'd usually date. Let's just let this be what it was and not make things worse."

My heart was pounding so hard, it was a bloody miracle I didn't crack a rib. "What do you mean make things worse?"

She started pacing in a tight loop, her gaze averted. "Liam, this, this thing with us isn't something I do. I don't know what you expect, but I know the time will come when the differences between us will only drive us apart. I can't..." She paused and shook her head sharply, her eyes finally swinging to mine. "I don't do things like this. I'm not...Oh, I don't know how to explain."

My heart literally ached as I stared at her. I didn't understand what she meant, but a sense of desperation was building inside of me. "Olivia, what happened? Why are you doing this?"

She stopped her pacing and stared at me, her cheeks flushed and her eyes dark. "Because I'm in over my head. You act like you don't know what I mean, but you have to. I mean, my God, you have some amazing model from Britain visiting you here! That's not me. My career is what matters to me, and I'll be lucky if I haven't already messed that up. You'd never have even noticed me if you hadn't ended up here for your surgery."

I shook my head, trying to make sense of what she meant. "What woman are you talking about?" The only woman I could think of was Millie Morton who annoyed me to no end and had stopped by to visit the team the other day. She'd dated half the guys on my old team back in London and was constantly flaunting her assets to all of us. But she certainly hadn't been here to see me.

Olivia's eyes whipped up. "Liam, there was a picture online," she said, her tone almost withering.

A flash of anger raced through me. Not with Olivia, but the situation. Anger that all it took was some random photo I didn't even know had been taken to give Olivia a reason to question us. "If you're talking about Millie Morton, she bloody well wasn't here to see me, and she takes every chance she can get to drape herself on anyone. I didn't think anything of it because she's annoying as hell. I don't know exactly what photo you're talking about, but I haven't a damn thing to hide when it comes to Millie. I barely know the woman and prefer to keep it that way."

Olivia waved a hand dismissively and turned partially away. "It doesn't really matter. I need to get my mind back where it needs to be, and not worry about stuff like this. Our lives are so different it doesn't even make sense for us to be together."

To hell with letting her keep her distance. I strode to her and tried to pull her into my arms, but she stiffened. When I looked down, her eyes collided with mine, bright with tears. "Olivia, please..." I tried to hold her close, but my arms fell away when she stepped back abruptly.

"I can't. I can't keep being so stupid. It's bad enough I put myself in a position to lose my job. I can't keep going along because I'm already in too deep. Please just go." She stepped away and turned her back to me, her arms wrapped tightly around her waist again.

I couldn't go, not when I felt like my heart was being ground to dust. "What do you mean you're in too deep?"

She turned back and smiled a sad little smile. "I think perhaps we're in different places because we're different people. You showed up and swept me off my feet, almost literally. Meanwhile, you can have your pick of women and they're betting on you back in London, all because you're famous for never committing to anyone. Let me do this. I'd like to at least keep my pride."

Another flash of anger rose inside of me. It infuriated me to have her belittle what we had like this and make it seem as if it was nothing more than a fling. At that moment, there was a soft knock on her open door. Olivia strode swiftly to the door. "Dr. Adams, I didn't know you were stopping by."

I recognized the director's name and slowly turned. The woman who stood in the doorway was tall and willowy with short gray hair. She wore a white lab coat over black slacks. Her eyes flicked in my direction and back to Olivia. If she thought anything about me being there, her expression was controlled.

"I was hoping to speak with you for a few minutes. I can come back if you'd like," Dr. Adams said.

I wanted to shout that she should absolutely come back later after I'd had time to convince Olivia she needn't shut me out of her life. But I knew that would anger Olivia, so I stayed quiet.

"Oh, that's not necessary. I'm just finishing up with..." She paused, and I realized she was trying to decide how to address me. I forced myself to hold my tongue, though I almost had skid marks on it. "...Mr. Reed," she finally finished.

So I was back to being Mr. Reed. Bloody hell. I swallowed, the only thing keeping me from stalking to Olivia and pouring my jumbled feelings into a kiss was the presence of Dr. Adams.

Dr. Adams glanced to me, nodding slightly. "Mr. Reed. I hear from Tim your rehab is going quite well. I do hope you've felt supported here at the clinic."

The tension in the air was so heavy, it was almost suffocating. Olivia wanted me out of here and fast. Between that and the inherent awkwardness of her boss's knowledge of what had transpired between us, well, tense didn't quite capture how the room felt. I couldn't say I felt good at having put Olivia in this position, in fact I felt like hell over that part of it all. Yet, I'd have walked over hot coals to have her and didn't want to let go.

I inclined my chin and nodded in return toward Dr. Adams. "I couldn't ask for better care. Between Dr. Bowen and Tim, I won't be surprised if I'm stronger than I was before when I return to play."

Olivia kept her gaze studiously averted from me, but she wasn't budging from where she stood by the door. I could either make this situation much, much worse by trying to insist she keep talking with me, or I could leave and regroup. I called upon every ounce of grace my mother instilled in me and walked to the door, passing a little too close to Olivia. "I was on my way out, so I'll leave you two to talk." I paused at the door, looking straight at Olivia. "I'll be in touch."

I knew it was brazen to say anything in front of her director, but I bloody well didn't care. I had to force my feet to move. The office door closed behind me, and I kept walking, my heart sick and my stomach nearly chewing itself up.

Chapter Twenty-Six

OLIVIA

I walked quickly through the chilly drizzle, my head down and my eyes on the sidewalk. I didn't have to look up to know when I'd reached Desert Isle Café because the glow of light spilling from the windows glittered on the wet sidewalk. I was meeting Daisy for coffee. I'd almost backed out because I wasn't quite up for talking about Liam, but I needed reinforcements. Last night, I'd turned off my phone after the first text from Liam, only to wake up to a several more from him, ending with: *So you're not going to talk to me this way. Right then. I won't bloody give up.*

I didn't doubt for a second that Liam would show up at my apartment or office again. What I didn't understand was why he wouldn't just let it go. I wasn't stupid enough to think what lay between us wasn't powerful, but he had to realize it was smart to end things. I needed to get back to the life I used to have, the one where I took pride in my job and where the emotional tides of desire and need weren't swinging me back and forth inside. I breathed through the knot of pain in my chest and pushed through the door into Desert Isle. This was one of my comfort places, always warm, always welcoming, and relaxed enough I didn't have to worry about anything. A small sense of relief washed over me to be here. I saw Daisy already in a corner table with Harper and gave a quick wave as I headed to the counter.

Moments later, I slipped into the empty chair at the table and glanced between Daisy and Harper. "Hey there. Sorry I'm a few minutes late. I lost track of time while I was charting."

"Hey, for once you were later than me," Daisy said with a grin. "Harper, of course, was probably right on time."

Harper rolled her eyes. "The only reason I'm usually on time is because if I'm on this side of town, it's because I had a meeting somewhere other than my office. Anyway, how's it going?" she asked, her warm blue eyes on me.

I could tell Daisy must've filled her in, otherwise she wouldn't look so concerned. I didn't bother to sidestep and looked between them. "I'm fine, perfectly fine," I said, an edge of frustration in my tone. I'd been telling myself I was perfectly fine. My life would go right back to what it had been—drama free and without the emotional muddle of tripping and nearly landing on my face in my free fall dive into Liam.

Daisy had her coffee mug halfway to her mouth and set it down with a thump. "You are not fine. You look like hell. Liam tracked me down today too."

"What?!" I interjected, my eyes widening and my pulse leaping.

"If you'd bothered to call me today, I'd have filled you in," Daisy said with a thread of annoyance in her tone.

"I'm sorry. I *was* really busy at the clinic." Daisy had texted around noon, telling me she needed to talk to me. I'd fired off a quick reply that it would have to wait until tonight. "So what did he want?" I couldn't help the pitter patter of my heart, hope doing a little dance inside.

Daisy leaned back, her gaze softening. "Believe it or not,

he wanted my advice. I don't know what you said to him yesterday, but he's pretty upset about it. What happened?"

I didn't know what to think of the fact that my heart gave a little jump at hearing Liam was upset. It's not like I wanted him to be upset, but at least I wasn't alone in being a mess inside. I took a gulp of coffee, savoring the bracing flavor. "I guess I broke up with him. It's not like we were really together, but I told him we needed to stop."

Harper idly traced the edge of her mug and looked to me and then Daisy. "What did Liam say?"

"He said Olivia won't talk to him, and he wanted my help. I asked him how much Olivia mattered..." Daisy swung her eyes in my direction. "And he said she meant everything. That man is seriously into you. I might think it's stupid for you to wonder why he's into you, but I get worrying about the whole thing. I feel responsible for blowing this up by texting you about that photo. He said you mentioned it and then explained the whole thing. Context always matters. Give the guy a chance. He looks like a lost puppy, and I think he seriously had to check his pride to come talk to me. Not to mention he actually had to hunt me down."

"So what was your advice?" I finally asked. That stupid hope was running in circles in my heart to hear Liam had tracked Daisy down to ask her about me.

Daisy leaned back, her gaze speculative. "Not telling."

"Not fair," I said sullenly, taking a quick gulp of coffee.

Harper shook her head at Daisy. "Seriously?"

Daisy was unrepentant. "Seriously? I'm actually trying to be a good friend here. If there's one thing I know about you," her gaze swung to me "you've been way too committed to being alone. It's not like I gave away any secrets. I just gave the man who's so obviously in love with you a few pointers. That's all."

I stared at her, my heart drumming and my throat tight. To hear her so easily say Liam was in love with me did crazy things to me. Before Liam, my life had been tidy and calm.

Even if I was trying to convince myself that was best, it was hard not to miss him acutely every other second.

Harper's brows hitched up, and a low laugh escaped before she turned to me. "If there's one thing you can trust about Daisy it's that she'd kick Liam's ass if she didn't believe he was that into you. Maybe you should give him a chance."

I tried to shove away the hope blooming inside me. I couldn't let this sweep me right back into the foolish insanity. It was too overwhelming, too messy and made me feel out of control, which I definitely did not enjoy.

I wasn't up for debating the point with Daisy and Harper, so I glanced between them. "Nothing's going to change. He's a famous sports star with women drooling over him. I'm a doctor with a pretty boring life, all things considered." I took a sip of coffee and glanced to Daisy. "The photo was a good reminder of everything I'm not. That's Liam's life, not mine."

My throat tightened and tears pressed at the back of my eyes, so I drained the rest of my coffee and stood to get a refill. I didn't want to keep discussing Liam. I wasn't getting the reinforcement I'd hoped for from Daisy and Harper. I wanted someone to tell me my choice made sense. I got another coffee and returned to the table. Harper glanced up and looked as if she might say something, but instead she looped her arm over my shoulders and gave me a squeeze. When Daisy started to say something, Harper shook her head firmly as her arm slid off my shoulder. "Not now."

Daisy gave her a hard stare and shrugged. Conversation moved on topics that had nothing to do with Liam. By the time I left a while later, I felt slightly lighter inside, if anything because I'd had a little time where my thoughts managed to temporarily skip off the groove of Liam deepening in my mind.

Hours later, I lay in bed, my eyes wide open and the ache of missing Liam keeping me awake.

Chapter Twenty-Seven

LIAM

"What the...?!" My last word was choked off by the towel slapping against my face.

I grabbed it and yanked it off, promptly tossing it right back at Alex. "What the hell?" I asked, finishing my question this time.

Alex caught the towel and flung it into the hamper before leaning against the doorframe and crossing his arms. He'd just finished showering and his hair was damp and sticking up in a rumpled mess. That didn't detract from his glower. When Alex was pissed, it showed. "Bloody tired of you moping around. Go talk to Olivia before I drag your sorry arse to her."

I glared at him and plunked down in a chair at the kitchen table. "I'm not bloody moping."

Alex shoved off the doorframe and sat down across from me, drumming his fingers on the table. "Aye, you are. Haven't see you crack a smile in days. Thought you went to find Daisy for a reason."

I swallowed against the tight feeling in my chest and

rolled my head side to side, trying to ease the tension knotted there.

"Daisy wasn't much help," I mumbled and ran a hand through my hair.

"What did she say?"

"She told me to go big or go home. Whatever the fuck that means." I shook my head slowly and sighed.

Alex eyed me. "What do you need? A point by point diagram, I suppose. Bollocks. You know what go big or go home means. If you're too dodgy to face Olivia, it's on you mate."

I threw another glare in his direction, though my gut turned with a sick feeling. I'd been frantic to see and talk to Olivia, but she'd blocked every avenue—not answering my texts, ignoring my knocking when I stopped by her apartment and conveniently being busy anytime I happened by the clinic. In desperation, I'd gone to see Daisy who hadn't exactly been helpful. She'd told me Olivia didn't let many people close after her parents died. Not a shocker. Then, she'd gone on to show me the stupid photo online of Millie with me.

I'd hardly been paying attention while I was waiting outside the stadium with a few teammates. Millie, per usual, had pranced about us. Just as I'd told Olivia, Millie hadn't been with me. Ever. But she'd done a damn good job of leading the British gossip rags around by the nose with scintillating hints. She'd taken every opportunity she had to drape herself all over me when we happened to be in the same place at the same time. While I'd be the first to admit I'd been happy to enjoy the women who threw themselves at me, I'd never had the slightest interest in Millie. She was too opportunistic, too greedy and too shallow for me.

I had to give Daisy credit for admitting she maybe should've taken a look at the next few pics online with Millie flirting with half the team. Daisy had looked appropriately chagrined, but it didn't change anything. "Look," she'd told me "maybe this set Olivia off, but this isn't easy for her. She's pretty well set in keeping her life calm. If you want to get her back, you're going to have to shake her up. If you want her to believe you love her and it's worth fighting for, you're gonna have to go big, or take your ball and go home."

Recalling Daisy's words, I looked over at Alex and fought the urge to squirm. His way too perceptive gaze held mine. "I'm not being dodgy," I mumbled.

"Well then, do something about it." He gave me a hard stare and shook his head. "You're due to play soon. Don't let this get in your head. Make it right."

At that, he shoved his chair back and stood, leaving me to stew in my own thoughts while he got ready for practice. I didn't like thinking about it, but I was worried I was letting this get me all mixed up in my head. I might not have the tidy, calm life Olivia did, but I hadn't had much experience with falling in love. Scratch that, I hadn't had any experience. I had to force myself to drag my arse off the chair and follow him.

I spent the afternoon trying to keep my head on straight and spinning over what the hell to do that would be big enough to knock through Olivia's barriers.

Chapter Twenty-Eight

OLIVIA

There was a soft knock at my exam room door before it opened. I looked over to see Dr. Monroe, the team doctor for the Seattle Stars stepping through the door with a patient. The patient in question was Mack Dawson, one of the American players on the team, a true-blue Seattle boy and handsome as all get out. Mack had a body to die for, shaggy blondish-brown hair and twinkling hazel eyes with a roguish smile. I looked at him with hope in my heart, hoping against all reason he'd elicit even a flicker of the attraction I felt toward Liam. Nothing, I felt nothing. I looked at Mack with a clinical eye, purely objective with not the slightest bit of interest. I'd developed this disconcerting habit of thinking I was going to look up and find Liam. Today was worse than usual because I'd known Dr. Monroe was coming along with Mack and couldn't help but wonder if Liam would take the opportunity to stop by.

No Liam. Only Dr. Monroe and Mack. I swallowed my disappointment and smiled politely at Mack. "Hello Mack, I understand your elbow had a nasty collision with the ground."

Mack threw that roguish grin my way and even added a wink. Clearly, the man was an incorrigible flirt. I couldn't help but remember the first time Liam had been in this room with me, just as flirtatious and naughty. Just thinking about the kiss he laid on me before he left sent a jolt of heat through me. I hadn't heard from Liam in over a week. He'd even given up on texting me. I'd thought I wanted the very thing he was doing, yet I hated it. I missed him so much it ached, and I was getting restless and needy with desire. I'd never been restless and needy in my life. I'd woken several times deep in the night with the sheets damp and my panties wet from dreams about Liam.

Focus, Olivia. Focus. Liam did what you asked. Move on.

I adjusted my glasses and glanced between Mack and Dr. Monroe. "I had a few minutes to review the scan you sent over, but let me look again," I said, picking up my computer tablet and clicking to the screen. "It looks like an ulnar shaft fracture. I see they've already iced you and stabilized it temporarily." I set my tablet down and nodded toward Mack's arm.

Mack nodded. "It was like a bad dance. I got tangled up with a defender. He fell, I fell and my elbow got twisted."

"How much pain are you in?" I asked, fighting to keep from grinning. Mack might not do a thing for me in terms of attraction, but he was impossible not to like. He had an amusing, jovial way of talking and seemed entirely unbothered by the situation.

Mack shrugged again. "Not too much. I mean, it hurts, but I wanted to keep playing. Coach dragged me off."

I looked to Dr. Monroe. The injury was minor by any standard and certainly didn't require my expertise. I started to say as such, but Mack cut in.

"I know it's not much, but I want you to take care of it. After seeing how Liam's doing, I don't want to bother with anyone but the best," Mack said firmly.

The mere mention of Liam's name sent my pulse skittering wildly and flutters twirling in my belly. I swallowed and batted Liam out of my mind. I slid my gaze to Dr. Monroe who was standing slightly behind where Mack was leaning against the exam table. Dr. Monroe shrugged and threw me a slight grin.

It wasn't that I didn't take minor cases like this, but it was rare. I knew, however, the clinic would want me to take any case requested by the Seattle Stars. I looked back to Mack and nodded. "I'd be happy to cast your elbow, although you must know your injury won't require surgery and your rehab will be brief."

Mack grinned again. "Sounds good to me, Doc."

The conversation quickly turned to planning with Mack departing the exam room for an x-ray in order for me to set the bone this afternoon.

After Mack left the room, Dr. Monroe sent me spinning inside again by mentioning Liam. "Liam is due to play again next week. He started practice this week and hasn't missed a beat. We can't thank you enough for such a good outcome," Dr. Monroe said.

I adjusted my glasses and managed a nod, scrambling to keep my wits about me. "I'm glad to hear it." Questions tumbled through my mind, all of them entirely inappropriate to ask Dr. Monroe. I was relieved when my pager beeped. I checked the number and returned the call quickly.

I managed to skirt the topic of Liam through the remainder of the appointment, quickly casting Mack's forearm and sending him off to schedule with the rehab team. I hated the fact that anything that had a passing connection to Liam sent my mind racing along the loop dedicated solely to him in my brain. I walked home in the falling darkness, the evening absent of rain, which almost annoyed me because a rainy, gray day would've suited my mood better.

What would usually be a routine of comfort—making hot chocolate with a generous dash of Irish cream liqueur, settling down on the couch with a blanket draped over my legs, and the TV rumbling in the background while I finished up charting—felt lonely. I washed my single mug and plate from stale leftover pizza and set them in the dish rack before bursting into tears at the sight. Single every-thing. Single mug, single plate, single me. Liam had done just as I asked, and it hurt so badly I could hardly breathe at moments.

Chapter Twenty-Nine

LIAM

My phone buzzed in my pocket as I walked beside Alex. He'd dragged me down to the harbor, insisting I needed to go somewhere other than the flat and the stadium. I hadn't the heart for much else since Olivia had shut me out. I'd rejoined the team for practices in the lead up to a game next week and was doing my bloody best to keep my head in the game. Alex loved the ocean and was wont to drag me to the sea when we used to live back in London. Back there, we had to drive out of London to reach the sea. Our flat here was mere blocks away. We were presently walking along the docks at a harbor. Even at this early hour, the area bustled with energy with gulls swooping and calling, fishermen readying boats to leave, voices carrying across the water as the day began, and the low rumble of engines in the water.

I pulled my phone out of my pocket to see my dad's number flashing on the screen. "I'll take this," I said to Alex. He merely nodded, hands in his pockets as he stared out over the harbor.

Before I got a word out when I answered, my dad spoke. "Good day, Liam!" he said, a cheery tone to his voice.

Given that he'd had the roughest few months of us all since mum died, my heart clenched. "Good day to you, Dad. How are you?"

"Fine thanks, and you? How's the knee?"

"Much better," I said, my mind instantly cartwheeling to Olivia.

"Truly?" he asked.

I could hear the hopefulness in his voice and knew he'd been worried about me. He'd called a few times since my injury. While I'd been worried about him, he'd likely been just as concerned for me. "Truly, Dad. I'm back practicing with the team, and I'll be playing in our game next week."

Alex started walking ahead, so I followed behind at a slower pace. "How are things for you? Really?" I asked. I couldn't quite bring myself to state the painfully obvious, that mum had been gone going on months now. My parents had been lucky and loved each other to the end.

"I'm okay, Liam. I miss your mum, and I always will. I'm getting used to being dragged out and about by half the world between your brothers and our friends. But I'm okay. Truly."

My throat tightened as I imagined my father being dragged out of the house just to cheer him up. It was odd to think about mum just now. I hadn't realized it, but I'd gradually begun to adjust to her absence, which was a shift because I'd felt like kicking and screaming at first. Much as I'd had mixed feelings about signing with the Seattle Stars at first, I supposed the abrupt change of locale might've actually helped me. Hearing dad's voice and thinking of my mum just now sent a sharp stab of grief straight to the heart.

I cleared my throat. "I'm glad. Tell me how Carter and Leo are?"

My dad chuckled. "Carter's got 'imself a new girl who's a bit too busy for my taste. She'll be gone before we know it. Leo's working like a dog as usual. Tell me how you are. You don't sound quite right."

I took a deep breath, savoring the briny ocean air. Alex had turned along another dock, so I followed at a distance. My dad was too perceptive. I wasn't certain if I didn't sound quite right because the call with him brought up mum in my mind, or the ever-present pang of missing Olivia. Dad was one of the few people I'd turn to for advice. He rarely interfered, but he was clear and perceptive. "I don't?" I hedged at first.

"You don't. I've been reading the Seattle papers though and saw that silly Millie was in town."

Dad knew I hated the churning British gossips and had been beyond annoyed by Millie's machinations last year. Before I managed to reply, he continued. "And who is the woman you took to dinner? It'd do you good to find a nice girl," he said gruffly.

Leave it to my father to find a way to keep tabs on me. He was quite protective and had been known to chase off reporters if they tried to pump my family for info. His question about Olivia sent a pang through me. I'd yet to sort out what to do, and Alex had made his displeasure clear. He thought I was a coward, and I supposed I was. It was just that I was floundering with this. The challenge of Olivia had given me something to chase. Yet, I hadn't counted on love factoring into the equation, which had thrown me off.

"Liam? You still with me?" my father asked.

"I'm here, Dad. Millie's a bloody pain in the arse. I'll ignore her just as I did before. I'm certain she's getting paid to attend the game next week, some bullshit publicity stunt."

"Right. Tell me something I don't know though. Millie's antics aren't what's got you sounding so down."

I cleared my throat and gulped in air again. Alex walked beyond the end of the docks and aimed back toward downtown with a glance over his shoulder to see if I was still behind him. I gave a wave and thought about how to explain Olivia to my dad. "You're right. Millie's nothing to me. I met a girl, and I don't know what to do about her," I said bluntly.

"Ah. Is that it then?"

"Yes, Dad. I just said as such," I said, a hint of irritation threading my tone.

"Tell me about her."

"She's the surgeon who operated on my knee. She, uh..." I ran out of words. How to describe Olivia? She was lovely with her wild dark curls, her bright green eyes, her creamy complexion, and her sweet curves. I pictured her that first day I saw her, adjusting her glasses with her hair pulled back and a few curls merrily escaping her bun. In truth, the powerful desire she elicited was only scraping the surface of all she'd become to me. Her warmth, her brilliance, her strength of conviction, the fact she didn't even care about what so many others did as far as my status as a footballer, and just *her*. I missed her so, and I desperately needed to find a way to win her back...to go big.

"She means something to you," my dad said, his words interrupting my reverie.

"Yes. She does," I said simply. "I mucked it up though, and I don't know how to fix things with her."

"Do you love her?" my dad asked, his question simple and direct like the man he was.

I kept walking, my eyes on Alex ahead of me. We were away from the harbor now, walking along the busy street that led to our flat. My heart gave a hard kick at my dad's question, as if nudging me to face the truth. With my heart banging a swift staccato, I managed a breath and let it out slowly.

"I do. I love her," I finally said.

"What's her name?"

"Olivia." Saying her name sent a pang of longing through me.

"If you love Olivia, then you make it right," my dad said.

"I don't know how."

"Liam, you do know how. If you love her, you just need to think on it. You will find the right way. I'll say this though.

You're my oldest boy and you've always had a good heart. Your mum was worried about you because she fussed your career would get in the way and send women like Millie after you. If you're not sure what to do, think on it and it will come to you."

I swallowed against the tightness in my throat and nodded, realizing as I did my dad couldn't see me. "Dad, I haven't done this before. How would I...?"

"Liam, none of us knew how to do love until we did it. I don't know your Olivia, but I know you. You've a big heart and there's room to figure this out. Don't think too hard."

"Okay," I said, my voice sounding distant to me.

"Love you, son. I'll be watching the game. I'll fly to visit soon to meet your Olivia. Okay?"

"Okay. Love you, Dad. I'll sort this out. I will," I said, my voice sounding stronger than I felt.

The line clicked off, and I slowly slipped my phone back into my pocket. Glancing ahead, I saw Alex had stopped at the intersection before our flat and was leaning against a sign pole, his hands in his pockets as he stared up at the sky. With nothing other than Olivia on my mind, I jogged to meet him. One thing I loved about Alex was quiet came easy with him. He simply inclined his head and arched a brow when I reached him. The light changed, and we crossed the intersection.

The team had interviews this evening, prearranged months ago by management. If there was one thing I didn't enjoy about football, it was the media circus that went along with it. I'd had this fleeting hope it would be less so in America because here they couldn't keep the sport straight, but with the Seattle Stars an up and coming team in the international ranks along with a few other American teams, the media attention was rising. With Olivia filling my brain, for once I didn't care about the interviews. I'd get through the bother and sort out what to do.

I was home with rain falling in sheets outside, glittering on the windows as it rolled down the glass. My day at work had been longer than usual with an emergency surgery thrown in the mix. I'd walked home in the rain, and unlike a few weeks ago, Liam hadn't surprised me at the door even though I'd been wishing he had. My quiet evenings were chafing for me now. What had once been comfortable held an echoing emptiness. It was my life, the very life I'd had and been perfectly content to continue before I met Liam. In such a short span of time, he'd turned my world upside down. I wondered if I'd keep wishing not to be so lonely until I met someone else. Yet, I doubted anyone could fill the Liam-shaped hole in my heart. No one else would do. Daisy had declared I should go to Liam myself since it was obvious I was so miserable. However, the fact that he'd heeded my request to leave me alone spoke volumes. That and the underlying truth of how different our worlds were reminded me it was best if I moved on and found a way to let go.

I sipped my hot chocolate, liberally doused with Irish

cream liqueur, and opened my laptop. With a flick of the TV remote, I scrolled through the channels to find the best background for me while I worked, settling on a news show. A while later, I'd wandered off on a tangent and was scrolling through the website for the local animal shelter. This had occurred on the heels of a sharp pang of loneliness when my fingertips, which were plagued with a mind of their own, had clicked around online looking for news about Liam. I secretly did this even though I hated that I couldn't seem to resist. I would stare at pictures of him and miss him so much, it was a visceral pain. I came across a photo of him after a game in Seattle, shortly before I'd met him at the clinic. He was standing on the sidelines, his black hair mussed with a streak of dirt on his leg, his body emanating strength and power even when he was doing nothing other than standing in one place. It felt as if he was looking right at me, his blue eyes piercing as he stared at the camera. A jolt of longing hit me, so hard I had to catch my breath.

Abruptly, I determined I'd find a pet to keep me company. Perhaps then I wouldn't feel so lonely. I was presently reading the description of a cute dog with one ear that flopped down and another standing up. The dog in question was a male of indeterminate breed named Bentley. He was brown all over and on the small side. I'd never taken advantage of this benefit, however the clinic had an on-site doggy daycare for employees started years ago by one of the founders who loved to bring his dog to work. If it weren't for that, I couldn't even consider a dog because my work life didn't fit the needs of a dog. Bentley's sweet brown eyes called to me. I quickly fired off an email, selecting an appointment time from their website calendar. I'd be meeting Bentley tomorrow at noon.

My phone buzzed on the coffee table, indicating a text. I ignored it, reasoning I needed to get back to work. Seconds later, it buzzed and buzzed and buzzed. I finally grabbed it and saw Daisy had been texting. A call from her came through as I started to read her texts. I answered immediately.

"Good grief! What is it?" I asked.

"Channel 4!" Daisy practically yelled in my ear.

"What are you talking about?"

"Oh my God. Go to channel 4 on the TV."

"Why?"

"Just do it," Daisy said, her exasperation evident.

I snagged the remote off the coffee table and switched to channel 4. Liam was on screen talking with an interviewer. His friend and fellow teammate, Alex, was a few chairs away, along with several other men I presumed to be players on the Seattle Stars. I couldn't have changed the channel if my life depended on it, but I was almost angry Daisy made me see this. I didn't need to dwell on Liam.

"Why are you making me watch this? I need to move on, not watch him on TV."

"I'm hanging up. Listen and don't you dare change the channel."

The line went dead in my ear. I let the phone drop and tapped the button to turn up the volume. Despite part of me screaming for me to stop, I couldn't. I had to hear Liam's voice.

The interviewer was a woman with blonde hair, coiffed perfectly into a glossy bob that swung about her shoulders. Her eyes were locked onto Liam. "Well, Mr. Reed, as I'm sure you're aware, Millie Morton will be on hand for the exhibition game next week. Are the rumors across the pond true?"

Liam shifted in his chair and rolled his shoulders. He wore a navy button down shirt and faded jeans. His eyes were bright under the lights of the set. Even though he was surrounded by several other sexy soccer players, my mind barely registered their presence.

Liam eyed the interviewer, his gaze slightly annoyed. The pause between her question and his answer began to stretch, and I wondered what he might say. He cleared his throat, a hint of nervousness rising in the back of his eyes. How I knew that I couldn't say, yet I could feel it.

"Actually no. Those rumors are nothing more than that. I've never even been on a date with Ms. Morton, nor considered it. She chooses to create a different impression, one that's entirely untrue," he finally said.

The interviewer's eyes widened and she leaned back in her chair, angling her head to the side as if this was a serious matter. Meanwhile, my heart was beating like a drum, and my breath had gone shallow. "Is that so? How come you never chose to clear this up before?"

Her question had a tone of disbelief as if Liam was trying to fool her. His eyes narrowed. "Because it wasn't worth it, but now it is. I've never bothered to address the rumors about my personal life because I find it distasteful that anyone asks. But I won't stand by and allow Ms. Morton to perpetuate the false narrative she allowed the gossip pages to create. I've never been involved with her and never will. My heart belongs to another now and always will."

His words hit me like a bolt of lightning, and I almost dropped my hot chocolate. The interviewer's eyes widened, and she leaned forward in her chair. "Is that so? I don't suppose you'll let our audience know who that may be? Is it someone you left behind in London?"

Liam shook his head and shifted in his chair again. Tears were hot against the back of my eyes. He looked right at the camera. "I'll choose not to give her name because no one deserves to be hounded by the gossip rags. She's not in London. She's right here in Seattle, and I love her."

My phone was buzzing again and again and again, Daisy's name flashing on the screen. I ignored it and stared at Liam. I didn't hear much of anything else that was said as the interviewer asked a few more questions of Liam and moved on to speaking with the others players. Liam's eyes were locked to the camera, and mine were locked to the screen. I leapt up from the couch.

Chapter Thirty-One

LIAM

I sat on that damn interview platform set up at the stadium with my heart pounding and nearly sweating through the bloody button down shirt I'd been forced to wear for this group interview. I'd always hated this part of being a footballer. I loved to play and loved to work toward bringing whatever team I was on to the pinnacle of their performance, yet the publicity drove me nearly mad. I hadn't thought ahead about the interview and had distantly heard the guys joking about Millie in the locker room the other day. My mates from London, Alex, Ethan and Tristan, all knew I'd never had anything to do with her. Yet, the guys here in Seattle were still just getting to know us after we'd been traded to the Stars. I was so miserable over missing Olivia and trying to think of what to do to win her, to make her understand how much she meant to me that my usual annoyance about the bloody stupid machinations of Millie didn't even rise. It never occurred to me the interviewer would bring her up.

Here I was now, on the heels of publicly announcing I was in love with someone, and I didn't even know if Olivia had heard it. Brilliant planning on my part. That was the problem with me when it came to Olivia. I lost all ability to plan. I played the most strategic position in football as an attacking midfielder, better known as the playmaker. Everything I did in play revolved around me functioning essentially as the brain of the entire team, orchestrating our attack and distributing the ball accordingly. I had to think under pressure at all times and shift gears in a flash. When my mates didn't know what to do with the ball, it landed with me. All of my natural skill with quick thinking went out the window when it came to Olivia. I could hardly think. I somehow got through the rest of that bloody interview. Alex's eyes caught mine at one point when I apparently ignored a question. He stepped in and saved me by answering. Damn good thing because I'd entirely lost track of what was being said.

Finally, fucking finally, the interview ended, and we were escorted off the interview set and behind the cameras. Alex leaned close to me ear, his voice low. "Well, mate. *That* was big. Buckle up because you just set the gossips salivating."

I glanced to him, my eyes wide. "Bloody hell."

His eyes widened as we kept walking down the hall, being escorted quickly to the locker room. Coach had scheduled a meeting. I was tired from a grueling practice this morning and now emotionally drained from my impromptu declaration during the interview.

"Uh, so you didn't plan that back there?" Alex asked, his question nearly lost in the shuffle of footsteps echoing on the concrete floor of the hallway.

"Hell no. It just happened. I didn't even think about what it might mean as far as the whole publicity thing. Fuck. Olivia isn't going to like that. Not one bit."

"You didn't say her name, so that should keep them at bay for a bit, but it'll be like hounds on a scent. You might want to call her," Alex said.

There was a sudden pause in our walk down the hall. Our

teammates in front of us parted like water giving way, angling to one side of the hallway. I was looking at the floor, obsessing over what to say to Olivia because I'd just gone and created a potential mess for her. She was a private person. I knew she wouldn't want the manufactured drama. All I wanted was her, not the whirlwind of the entire sports media machine commenting on us. I also didn't even know if *us* was an option yet.

Alex nudged me with his shoulder. I ignored it and kept walking, but he almost punched me next. "What the hell?" I asked, glancing over at him. Alex stopped and lifted his chin forward. I followed his gaze and saw Olivia standing in Coach's office door. Coach stood beside her, his expression bemused. My feet stopped and I stood there staring at her, my heart pounding like mad. Her cheeks were flushed and her hair was damp. I dimly recalled it had been raining when we came back to the stadium for the interview. She appeared to have forgotten her raincoat as her cream-colored blouse was plastered to her skin and there were damp streaks on her charcoal gray leggings. My eyes caught on the fact her blouse was buttoned crookedly, as if she dressed in a hurry. All in all, she looked like a drowned rat. She was the most beautiful sight I'd ever seen.

I didn't realize I was frozen in place until Alex cleared his throat beside me. "Mate, you'd best move. Cameras are still rolling behind us."

When he gave me another hard nudge, I started walking and realized the rest of the team had moved onto the locker room. The only people left in the hallway were me, Alex and Coach, along with the bloody camera crew from the local TV station...and Olivia. Coach stepped away from Olivia and met me a few feet away. "You coulda given me a heads up about what you were planning. It's not a problem, but I've fielded calls from a few too many British reporters since you dropped your little news bomb. For now, I'll fend them off. My office is yours," he said in a low voice.

I caught his eyes. "Is she okay? I didn't mean..."

Coach closed his eyes for a moment. When he opened them, they held a twinkle as he shook his head. "Aw hell, you didn't plan this. Well, she started crying the minute she ended up in my office, so that's a good sign. That she's here says everything." He turned to the side and gestured to the camera crew. "Nothing more to see here," he called out. "Follow me." He slid a palm across my shoulders and nearly shoved me into Olivia. As soon as she stepped back into his office, I followed and the door slammed shut behind us.

I felt as if I'd just played an entire game, running hard the whole time. My breath came in deep gusts and my heart was kicking hard. The sound of echoing voices and footsteps faded as I stared at Olivia, my heart in my throat. She was soaking wet and shivering. Her gaze was bright, her eyes moist. We stood there, only a few feet between us, as quiet fell around us. A tear rolled down her cheek, and I closed the distance. I didn't know what she was feeling or thinking, but I couldn't see her in pain. I wrapped her in my arms and sighed as she softened against me.

I didn't know what the hell to say and was a bit relieved she didn't start talking right away. It felt so good to hold her. I stroked a palm in slow passes down her back and dipped my head into the curve of her neck, closing my eyes and breathing her in. After a moment, I felt the subtle shivers running through her and lifted my head. "You're cold."

Brilliant start to the convo. You've just admitted to the world you're in love and the woman in question is finally in your arms after far too many days apart and that's what you say?

I ignored my internal critic because Olivia *was* clearly cold and she needed not to be. That and it helped for me to have something concrete to focus on. I glanced around Coach's office for anything to help dry her off, my eyes landing on a stack of towels in the corner. "Let me get you a towel. Hang on." I stepped away and quickly snagged a towel, sending the entire stack in a tumble to the floor.

Ignoring the mess and not thinking much other than I needed to be right back beside Olivia, I spun around and returned to her.

I began drying her with the towel, at which point I couldn't help but notice her nipples, taut under her damp shirt and the silk of her bra. My body tightened, lust cracking like a whip inside. As powerless as I was to control my instinctive response to her, now didn't seem the time. My eyes whipped up and collided with hers—the air around us instantly electrified. I swallowed and tore my eyes away, focusing on swiftly rubbing the towel up and down her arms.

"Liam," Olivia said softly.

My chest was tight, my heart was pounding like crazy, and I couldn't seem to figure out what to say or do. I almost couldn't meet her eyes because, well, I supposed I was a bit afraid. The day she'd said she was in too deep with me felt like eons ago at this point. There was nowhere left to fall, I was well and truly in love with her. Funny, but I'd never thought of myself as a man who lacked in courage, but then I'd never faced anything like love. I gathered every ounce of courage I had and lifted my eyes again. Her lovely green eyes were waiting. I could tell she'd been crying as Coach had mentioned. Her eyes were a tad puffy and glistening with the sheen of tears. Yet, they held warmth and understanding and a hint of the very uncertainty I was swimming in. I relaxed a bit inside and managed to take a breath.

"Yes, luv?" I finally asked, the endearment I'd only ever used seriously with her rolling out of habit.

We stood together in the center of Coach's office with my hands on her arms, gripping the towel. She was damp and rumpled, her dark curls beginning to dry in their wild way. I was in my silly interview button down and still sweaty from announcing I was in love. Her shoulders rose and fell with a slow breath. "How are you?" she asked.

A pained laugh rumbled in my chest, and I shrugged. "I haven't been so good. I've missed you terribly, and I didn't know how to fix things. I, uh, don't know if you heard what I just went and said..."

"Oh, I did. That's why I'm here. I missed you too. I didn't know, well..." The uncertainty in her gaze deepened and she swallowed. "I suppose I should clarify if you were speaking of me during that interview."

My heart felt as if it was going to explode, but I managed to nod, and on the heels of a breath, to speak. "It could never be anyone but you."

Her breath caught, and her eyes teared up. "Oh, okay. That's good," she offered with a small smile. "I'd feel more than silly running down here if it was someone else."

I shook my head, starting to gain a bit of equilibrium inside. Olivia likely wouldn't have run through the rain just now if she weren't in love with me. I didn't know how love worked because I'd never been in love. I knew it to be entirely impossible to fall out of love with her, but I didn't know if the love she felt matched mine, or been mere infatuation that had dissolved in the weeks since we'd spoken. I surprised myself by managing to speak again. "Right then. Well, I'd feel quite silly announcing on the telly I was in love, only to find out it was all for naught."

She stepped closer, shaking her head slightly. "It's not all for naught. I've been falling in love with you since the day we met." She lifted a hand to rest on my chest, the heat of it just above my heart, which was truly about to crack a rib at this rate.

"I don't suppose you could tell me where you are in the falling bit," I managed with a half-smile. Humor had always been my refuge and would be now even when I was swamped in emotion.

Her lips quirked. "I fell all the way."

The hollow feeling that had subsumed itself inside of my heart eased, and I could breathe for the first time in weeks. Olivia started fiddling with the buttons on my shirt, and I suddenly realized she seemed to be set on unbuttoning them. I let the towel go from her shoulders and caught her hand in mine. While my body was more than happy to have her strip me right here, I didn't want her to think it was all about sex.

"What are you doing?" I asked gruffly, fighting the need rolling through me.

Her eyes held mine. "Taking your shirt off," she said pointedly. She swatted my hand away and carried on.

"Olivia. I love you. I don't want you to think it's..."

"All about sex," she finished for me. "I know it's not, but I missed you and I'm cold and I want you. You proved your point: sex is *never* boring with you," she said with a sly grin.

Then she shoved my shirt apart and ran her hands over my chest, and the thin thread of restraint I'd been hanging onto frayed and snapped. I laced a hand in her tangled hair and caught her lips, pouring weeks of longing into our kiss. We came together like a storm. She met me stroke for stroke, arching and flexing into me, her hands mapping my body roughly. I could feel the hard points of her nipples against my chest and tore my lips free. Our clothes came off, or rather half-off, in a blur. She was as greedy as me, yanking and tugging, her lips, teeth and tongue meandering about all the while.

With my shirt hanging apart and my jeans torn open, I found myself staring into her green gaze, dark with desire. Her legs were curled about my hips and her lush bottom gripped in my hands, barely propped on the edge of the desk. My cock rested at her entrance, its slick heat teasing me. I suddenly realized I didn't have a condom with me. Seeing as I hadn't planned any of this, that was one detail that wasn't a surprise. I gritted my teeth and forced myself to pull back.

"I'm sorry, luv, but I don't have a condom. Don't worry, I'll..." I meant to say I'd take care of her because I'd be damned if I'd let her walk out of that office without making sure she came, but she curled her legs tighter around me and cut right in.

"I'm on the pill. I have been all along because, well..."

"You're super prepared like that," I added, unable to resist a grin.

Her cheeks flushed as she nodded. "So?"

"Are you sure?" I asked. It was a flat miracle I didn't just sink right into her then and there, but this had to be her call.

She nodded swiftly, tightening her legs around me and yanking me to her. I surged inside her velvety clench, a rough groan escaping. Sweet hell. She felt so damn good—hot, wet and tight. My forehead fell to hers, and I held still, almost in awe of how it felt to be this close to her. Her breath was coming in sexy as hell breathy whimpers. She didn't let me rest long, as she began to roll her hips into mine. All of the need I'd been holding tight inside unraveled in a slow spiral. Deep surges into her slick channel, her nipples brushing against my chest, her gaze holding mine—all of it spinning together in a dizzying slow dance.

Her eyes fell closed and her channel throbbed around my cock as she cried out, and I finally let go, my release thundering through me and into her. Her head tipped forward into the curve of my neck with her breath coming in gusts against my skin. My own was heaving, but gradually slowed. I sifted through her damp curls and closed my eyes, savoring all that this was. I'd gone and lost my mind, but Olivia was here now and it would be okay.

She lifted her head, and I glanced down to meet her eyes. She reached up and traced my brows with her fingertip. We were still joined, and I hated to move even an inch away from her, but I knew reality would intrude soon. Coach had given us the small gift of privacy, but it wouldn't last. "I'm sorry I was such an idiot. It took me a bit to sort things out in my head."

She shook her head swiftly and traced my mouth with

her fingertip, sending a hot jolt of lust through me. Bloody hell. This woman got to me the way no woman ever had.

"You weren't an idiot. I was too, in my own way." Her gaze grew pensive. "So what now?"

Reality intruded in my mind, but I swatted it away. There was more than one now to focus on. "Well, tonight I'm staying with you and then probably every night after that forever. We'll sort out the details. So there's that. Then, there's the now-now."

Her lips quirked. "The now-now?"

"The 'I should be in a team meeting in the locker room now,' and the fact I just told the sports media I was in love, *and* you showed up here when the cameras were rolling. Even though I didn't mention your name, pretty sure the cat's out of the bag. That *now*." A fierce tenderness washed through me. I wanted to protect her from the media storm that would ensue. I was used to it, but I still hated it. Olivia wasn't, and she didn't deserve to have to deal with it.

Her eyes widened and then she burst out laughing, which oddly enough woke my cock right back up because with every gust of her laughter, her channel clenched around me. Her laugh slowed and she took a deep breath. "Oh, that *now*. I get it. I guess I didn't think about what it might mean to have me show up here." She shrugged blithely. "Oh well. I already told my boss, so we headed off that potential scandal." Her eyes turned earnest. "Don't worry. I can handle it. I'm really good at ignoring people, so that's just what I'll do."

My grin stretched from ear to ear. She *was* good at ignoring people, and she'd done her bloody best to ignore me back at the beginning. "Right. Ignore it. Best strategy ever."

There was a knock at the office door, and Coach's muffled voice came through. "Liam. We need you in a few minutes. Okay?"

Coach instantly became my favorite coach for reasons that had nothing to do with his actual leadership and coaching ability. The man knew how to let someone have some privacy. "I'll be out in five," I called out.

He didn't reply, but we could hear his footsteps retreat down the hall. I glanced to Olivia. "I have to go."

"I know," she said with a grin as she shimmied her hips back.

We untangled ourselves and put our clothes back together. This time, she buttoned her shirt properly. I scanned the office and quickly put up the towels I'd knocked on the floor before turning to find her waiting at the door. I looked over at her, and my heart felt as if it might truly explode. She was standing by the door, all put together and tidy, nothing to let anyone know on the outside that she'd just been half-bare on the desk with her legs wrapped around me. I loved the contrasts of who she was. She looked a tad bit nervous, and it occurred to me she might be worried cameras were waiting outside.

I went to her and curled my hand around hers. "Coach will have chased them off. I can't promise they won't be outside, but I'll walk you out."

Chapter Thirty-Two

OLIVIA

My legs were draped over Liam's lap with one of his strong hands curled over my calf. We were sitting on my sofa, sipping coffees. I'd woken up beside him after he'd come to my apartment last night as promised and proceeded to leave me nearly boneless after licking, kissing and touching every inch of my body and sending me flying again and again. This morning, for the first time ever, I called out from work. Liam had practice later this afternoon, but I wanted the morning with him. He'd dashed off to pick up bagels from a bakery on the corner, and we'd had a lazy breakfast and coffee together. I suddenly remembered my appointment to meet Bentley.

"What time do you have practice?" I asked, wondering if I should still go visit Bentley or not.

"Two," he replied, his thumb stroking my calf and sending little shivers through me.

"Oh." I bit my lip, pondering what to do. "I have an appointment at noon, but..."

"For work?"

I shook my head. "No. Last night before, well, everything, I was lonely and thought maybe I should get a dog, so I looked up the shelter and scheduled an appointment to meet a dog. Maybe I should cancel, but I feel weird about that. I mean, I've always loved dogs and had one when I was little, but..."

"I'll go with you," he said firmly. "Dogs are splendid."

"Really?"

"Really," he said with a grin. "Luv, if you want a dog, you should get a dog."

A short while later, we stood inside a small fenced in yard. It was blessedly not raining today, and the woman at the shelter who seemed to be the meet and greet person had suggested we spend some time with Bentley outside in their play area. Bentley was even cuter in person than in his pictures. With one ear perpetually up and the other down, he looked almost comical. He was medium sized and brown all over from his eyes to his short and wavy fur. Bentley was friendly with a mellow personality and estimated to be about three years old. Liam was presently playing fetch with him. I wasn't sure who was more delighted with the activity—Liam or Bentley.

I didn't even ask, but left them to play and walked inside to the desk. "We'd love to adopt him. Tell me what we need to do."

The woman glanced up at me, immediately handing over a clipboard with forms to fill out. I must've looked surprised because she grinned. "I saw you holding him, and your boyfriend obviously loves him, so it seemed meant to be," she explained.

I quickly filled out the paperwork and paid a fee. I was pleased to learn Bentley had already been neutered and was up to date on all of his shots. After everything had been done, I asked, "Do we need to wait?"

"Sometimes we ask for a waiting period, but we'll waive it for you two."

My puzzlement must've shown on my face. She flushed

slightly. "Well, we're aware that's Liam Reed from the Seattle Stars, so it's not like we can't find him if there's a problem."

I flushed beet red, realizing this kind of thing might happen more often. She smiled apologetically. "I didn't mean to be weird. I don't really follow soccer, but my mom does, so I knew who he was. You must be the woman he was talking about last night."

My momentary discomfort passed. I'd have to get used to this, so I might as well start now. "I am and don't worry about it. He'd be hard not to notice."

In short order, Liam and I were walking down the street with Bentley on a leash. Liam had offered to walk him, and in fact, seemed completely smitten with him. We paused at the corner where Bentley wagged at everyone who passed by. I looked up at Liam. "You seem to be pretty into getting a dog."

Liam glanced down and nearly took my breath away. His eyes were as blue as the sky and locked onto me. In a flash, it felt as if we were all alone, despite the fact cars and people were all around us. "I like dogs, and Bentley's splendid. It's not just that though. We're adopting him, so that means you're stuck with me. I take dog ownership very seriously," he said, closing the distance between us and snaking his arm around my waist. Flush against him, my pulse took off and I wondered how I'd gotten so lucky.

EPILOGUE

Liam

I stood on the sidelines, my breath heaving and energy coursing through me. Even at the end of a game when I was worn out, I felt energized. I rested my hands on my hips and glanced around for Alex. He'd just given us a shut out against the other team, cleanly blocking every shot they had. I finally found him standing beside Coach with a few of our teammates surrounding him. Per usual, Alex looked entirely unmoved by the moment. Just another day's work for him. Meanwhile, he was getting clapped on the back, and everyone in his immediate vicinity looked overjoyed.

I wove through the team to his side. "Well done," I said with a nod when I caught his eyes.

Alex cracked a grin. "That it was. Great play today. As usual, you led a bloody brilliant offense."

I rolled my eyes. "Can't take any credit, can you? Not throwing shade at the rest of us, but we won because you made sure they didn't score."

Alex shrugged. "Right then." He looked past my shoulder, another grin stretching across his face.

"What?" I asked.

"Here comes your girl," he replied, his eyes flicking to me and away again. "Hey Olivia."

I felt Olivia's presence behind me as soon as he spoke. I turned just as she reached my side, slipping her hand through the crook of my elbow. "Hey Alex. Great game as usual." She caught my eyes and leaned up to kiss my cheek before turning back to Alex. "I never know exactly what to say to you after a game like this because it's all about what you made *not* happen," she said with a grin.

Alex shrugged. I glanced down at Olivia. "He's bloody awful at taking a compliment."

She smiled up at me, her green eyes bright in the crisp air. Just like that, nothing more than a smile from her while my teammates bustled around us and the stadium noise rumbled with the crowd filing out of their seats, and my heart clenched. The air around us heated as if lit by a flame. My body tightened and I leaned forward, about to kiss her, when Alex cleared his throat. I glanced back to him, arching a brow. Alex merely nudged his chin to my other side where I saw a cameraman approaching with his camera trained on Olivia and I. Instead of a kiss, I leaned down to whisper in her ear.

"Later, luv." I couldn't resist dropping a quick kiss in the delectable curve of her neck. As soon as I lifted my head, the cameraman and an interviewer from a sports channel were upon us. Thanks to the focus on Alex's shut out, I got away with only a few questions and managed to keep Olivia's hand firmly in mine the entire time.

I was in the thick of my second season with the Seattle Stars. We were on track to win our division this year. After we got through the after game interviews, I made my way to the locker room, reluctantly leaving Olivia to wait. She assured me she'd meet me out front and pick up pizza for us. I showered in record time, my mind spinning back over the last year. The mess I'd felt inside after my mum's death, my move to the US and my knee injury felt like distant memories. I still missed my mum, missed her like crazy sometimes, but time had dulled its sharpness. As torn as I'd been about signing with the Stars at the time, I wouldn't change a thing now. I felt the same about my knee. Without those two events, I'd never have met Olivia. About now, she was the sun in my universe and everything that led to her was bathed in its glowing light.

I hurried out of the locker room, glancing over my shoulder when I heard a chuckle from Alex as I passed by his locker. "What?" I asked.

He'd been in the midst of pulling a sweatshirt on and tossed the hood back once it was over his head and shoulders. His brown eyes held a teasing gleam when he met mine. "Mate, it's a good thing Olivia's so good for you because you can never get to her fast enough."

I shrugged and grinned. "Bloody right about that. You'll find out someday," I said with a wink as I spun around and made my way down the long hallway that led outside. I pushed through the doors into the late afternoon sunshine. I found Olivia right away. She sat on a bench nearby with Bentley beside her, his leash looped around her hand and a pizza box beside her. She often brought Bentley to games with her because Coach was kind enough to let us leave him in his office during the actual game. I stopped where I was and just looked at Olivia.

She'd come to the game from the clinic with her hair pulled back in a tidy knot perched on top of her head and wearing a fitted black skirt and rich blue blouse, buttoned almost to her neck of course. I couldn't wait to take her hair down and tear her blouse apart. She was still working at the clinic and managing a waitlist of high-profile cases. She'd received a written reprimand from the clinic's board for her involvement with me. Dr. Adams had actually met with me and given me the option to file a complaint if I felt the need to do so. I'd burst out laughing and assured her it was entirely unnecessary. Even then, I'd been relieved at the outcome because I knew it had weighed on Olivia. She was by nature an honest person who played by the rules. I was happy to be the one who'd inspired her to break a few.

I suddenly realized I was stuck in place when someone bumped me as they walked by. Olivia had that effect on me —everything else fell away around her. I gave my head a shake and walked to her. Bentley leapt off the bench, his entire body wiggling when he saw me. "Bentley boy," I said as I knelt beside him to greet him.

I straightened when Olivia stood up. I hooked my arm around her waist, pulling her flush against me and fitting my mouth over hers when she opened it, presumably to speak. She gasped, and I took full advantage, sweeping my tongue inside and groaning when hers slid against mine. A low whistle nearby nudged me out of my haze, and I pulled back, looking down at Olivia. Her cheeks were flushed, pretty and pink, and her eyes were bright. "Hi," she said simply.

"Hello luv. That was for the kiss I didn't get right after the game."

She giggled and started to step back, but I held her firm. "Liam," she whispered fiercely, pausing to take a breath. "There's people everywhere, and you know any minute now someone will take another picture that will end up..."

"Online," I finished for her. "I don't give a bloody damn. I love you and I don't care if the whole world knows it."

Bentley nudged my knee. I glanced down and followed his gaze to see a photographer, likely from one of the sports news teams departing from the stadium, with his camera aimed right at us. I looked back to Olivia, gesturing over my shoulder. "There, see already done. Now let's go home, so I can have you all to myself."

I couldn't resist giving her bottom a squeeze as I slid my hand down to reach for hers. The flush on her cheeks deepened, and she stopped where she was, glancing up at me again. "Well, if we're going to be in the gossip pages again, we might as well give them something good."

My oh-so-proper fiancée slipped her hand around my neck and yanked me down for another kiss.

————

Thank you for reading The Play - I hope you loved Olivia & Liam's story!

For more steamy, sports romance, Alex & Harper's story is up next in Big Win. Alex doesn't lose control. Ever. Until he meets Harper. "...singe-worthy chemistry and intimacy..." Don't miss Alex's story!

Keep reading for a sneak peek!

Be sure to sign up for my newsletter for the latest news, teasers & more! Click here to sign up: http://jhcroixauthor.com/subscribe/

Alex

My breath came in steady gusts as I ran along the walkway. It was barely past dawn, my favorite time of day, and I was out for my morning run. The park was quiet as I followed the path along the shore. Gulls called in the distance, the only noise to speak of at this hour. I ran for a solid half hour and slowed to a walk as I made my way through the forested part of the park back to my flat. The air was cool and damp, typical for a spring morning in Seattle. A sudden burst of chatter from squirrels in the trees caught my attention, and I glanced up to see a woman walking toward me with a giant dog at her side. The dog almost reached the woman's shoulder, tall and stately, the dog walked with grace at her side. I didn't realize I'd stopped where I was until the woman got close enough for me to realize I knew her. The moment this realization dawned, a prickle of awareness ran up my spine.

Harper Jacobs was a good friend of my best mate's fiancée. Harper also got to me—big time. I couldn't put my finger on why. She was attractive, but in an understated way. I'd met her a bit ago when Liam, the best mate in question, invited me to meet him for coffee. Harper was there with Liam's fiancée Olivia. I'd encountered her a few more times since then, seeing as we shared best mates in a way. She was polite and friendly, but she always seemed to have an invisible bubble around her. I wanted to know why she kept herself protected behind that. I waited for her to reach me, which she eventually did. She slowed to a stop, rested her hands on her hips and glanced up at me.

"Alex, right?" she asked.

"That would be me. I see you're out for a walk," I said, instantly wondering why I couldn't have slightly better conversational skills. Stating the obvious wasn't particularly inviting. I usually didn't give a bloody damn about conversing, but I wanted to know Harper.

Harper nodded, her deep blue eyes crinkling at the corners with her small smile. "I am. I'm going to guess you're just finishing a run," she replied with a nod to my feet, which were encased in running shoes.

"That I am. I come here almost every day. I think I'd have seen you before if you're here often, what with...?" My words trailed off as I gestured to her giant dog.

"Stanley," she filled in, her smile stretching.

Damn. I wished I could see her smile more. Her whole face lit up and that careful, controlled look in her eyes softened.

As if in response to his name, Stanley stretched his head to my hand and slowly sniffed it. After a moment, he dipped his head further, nudging it under my hand as if he expected me to pet him. So I did. He was easily taller than my waist, his large eyes blue and his fur dappled steel gray.

"He likes you," Harper said. "Stanley can be picky, so take that as a compliment."

I stroked his head slowly and looked over at Harper. Her glossy brown hair was pulled back in a ponytail high atop her head with loose locks escaping. She blew a breath, effectively blowing one lock of hair out of her eyes. She wore fitted leggings and a fitted top, both bright blue, which brought out her eyes. She was clearly in good shape, but also managed to be curvy at the same time with full hips and generous breasts. I realized I was staring at her and forced myself to recall what she'd just said.

"I'll take it as a compliment then. What kind of dog is he?"

"Great Dane. He's on the large side for the breed, but he's nothing but a gentle giant." Her eyes canted down, and she laughed softly. Stanley had taken another step closer to me and nuzzled his massive head against my hip. "He's a lover, not a fighter," she said, looking back up to me. "So you run here on top of your practices?" she asked, referencing my career as a goalkeeper for the Seattle Stars.

I was a Seattle transplant, traded here with three of my teammates from our old team in London. The Seattle Stars were America's current hot-shot football team. Though I still felt out of step with Seattle and America in general, none of it helped by the fact they insisted on calling football soccer here, I'd come to enjoy Seattle and the team. Being a professional footballer, or professional sports player of any kind really, meant you went where you were sent. Oh, there were negotiations and such, but that was the life. Well, that and dedicating your mind and body to a sport. I loved football and had loved it since I was a lad. I felt lucky to be able to play professionally.

I met Harper's clear blue gaze and nodded. "Most days I run on my own before practice."

She nodded, but was otherwise quiet. The silence started to stretch, but it was a comfortable silence. In the few times I'd been around Harper, we'd always been in a group, usually with our shared friends. It occurred to me just now that I didn't know much about her, other than who her friends were. Stanley nudged my hand, and I realized I'd slacked in petting him. "Sorry 'bout that, Stanley," I said, glancing down and stroking his sleek head again.

"I suppose you need to go," Harper said.

When I looked back at her, she looked, well the only way to describe it was nervous. Seeing as I hadn't a clue what she could be nervous about, I was flummoxed. But I didn't want her to go. I wanted to curl my hand around hers and walk through the park. I startled myself by saying so, or something along those lines.

"Why don't we walk for a bit?" I asked.

Her eyes widened for a beat, and her cheeks flushed. She went still, so still it worried me, and that controlled look slipped in front of her eyes again. Stanley took a step from me and nudged her hip gently before turning to stand close beside her. He exuded a quiet protectiveness toward her. Her shoulders rose and fell with a deep breath, and then she nodded. "Okay, that would be nice."

I simply nodded and turned alongside her. We began to walk with Stanley between us. He wasn't on a leash and didn't appear to need one. He stayed right by Harper's side and walked quietly, his gaze alert. Aside from the squirrels and birds chattering around us, it felt as if we were alone. Oh, there were a few other early risers out and about, but anyone here at this hour loved the quiet as much as I did. Harper was quiet as well. She idly kicked a pebble as we walked. I was torn between relief that we weren't face to face because Harper seemed more relaxed when I wasn't looking right at her and frustration because I wanted to look long and hard in her eyes and make the underlying worry and tension in her eyes disappear.

So I just kept walking. I didn't care to talk. Talking wasn't really my thing. As we walked along, I felt the hum of tension coming from Harper start to ease. Lincoln Park was an urban sanctuary and preserve situated by Puget Sound. There were the usual park amenities, such as a pool and tennis courts, but there was also a walkway along the beautiful shoreline and a well-preserved old growth forest, offering plenty of peaceful walking in the quiet hours of the day. We followed a footpath through the trees until we reached the walkway where I'd gone for my run this morning.

Salty air gusted off Puget Sound with the sun rising through the clouds. I glanced to the side when Stanley stopped abruptly. Stanley was staring straight ahead at a man running along the walkway. He didn't raise his hackles, nor did he make a sound, but it was plain he was bothered. I lifted my eyes to Harper. Splotchy red spread up her neck and face, and she looked absolutely horrified. She seemed to have forgotten I was there. I reached for her hand, which was curled in a fist at her side. The second I touched her, she swatted my hand away and then gasped.

"Oh, I'm sorry! I, um, I..." She looked from me back to the man, whoever the hell he was, running toward us. He was still a good distance away. I didn't know what was going on, but I had two inclinations—go punch the guy because his mere existence upset Harper, or get Harper away from him. Liam was wont to tease me for 'protecting the whole wide world' as he liked to put it. I didn't like seeing anyone hurt. Ever. I had my reasons, but those weren't particularly important now. What mattered was taking care of Harper.

"Harper?"

I wanted to reach for her hand again, but I didn't want to startle her as I already had. Her eyes flicked to me again. The blue had gone darker, but she held still. "I'm not sure what's up, but I think we should go," I finally said.

She nodded jerkily, but didn't move. So I reached for her hand, and this time she let me curl mine over hers. I don't know how long she'd been cold, but right now, her hand was freezing. Stanley was still staring at the man gradually closing the distance between us. I'd seen him running before and thought nothing of it. Whatever he was to Harper, it wasn't good. "Stanley, come on," I said softly as I turned and led Harper away.

The next few minutes were quiet. I didn't even notice the birds calling and squirrels chattering as we made our way back through the trees to the park entrance. I'd walked here, but I didn't know how Harper had arrived, nor did I know where she lived, but I wasn't leaving her side until she was home again. We reached the entrance, and I glanced down. Her skin was pale and her eyes shuttered. Stanley was as close as he could get to her on the other side without melding his body to hers.

After a moment, Harper looked up. "Did you walk here or drive?" I asked.

"I walked," she said, her voice low and quiet.

"Okay, where to?"

She looked confused. "I'm walking you home," I explained.

She started to shake her head, but I shook mine in return. "This isn't up for debate. You don't have to tell me what's got you so upset, but there's no bloody way I'm leaving you here with that look on your face. I'll walk you right to your door and you can slam it in my face, but I'm not letting you walk alone."

She swallowed and then nodded. "I live just a few blocks that way," she said pointing the same direction I'd walk to return to my flat. This area of Seattle was residential with a mix of homes and flats.

"Perfect. You must live a few blocks from me then. Shall we?"

At her small nod, I commenced to walk again, her hand still in mine. Her hand was finally starting to absorb heat from mine, which relieved me. I kept batting away thoughts about what may have put the stark fear in her gaze, but I didn't want to think about that now. I only wanted to make sure she got home. I pondered if I should offer to make her tea and almost laughed aloud. I was a true blue British boy. Tea was a daily part of my life and had been as long as I could recall. I drank coffee as well, but not much could beat a bad day the way a good cup of tea could.

I realized I hadn't been paying much attention to how fast I was walking. I tended to move quickly no matter the circumstance. I glanced to Harper, about to slow down, but she was keeping pace easily even if she still looked half-stunned. We crossed another street, and Harper slowed. My flat was another two blocks away. "It's here," she said, pointing up to an older home, clearly renovated into smaller flats. Flowers were blooming in abundance in boxes hung on windowsills and railings.

"I'll walk you in."

Her eyes gave little away, but she looked the tiniest bit relieved and nodded. After she keyed in a combination at the main entrance, which led into a massive foyer, we made out way up two flights of stairs that hugged the curved wall. I released her hand on the way up and stood beside her while she pulled her keys out of her jacket. They fell to the floor in a clatter. It appeared that each floor held a single flat with Harper's door the only one up here on the top floor.

"Dammit," she said in a whisper, promptly dropping them again when she tried to fit the key in the lock.

"Let me," I said, reaching down and scooping up the keys.

She was quiet while I slid the key into the lock. I felt entirely out of place and like I was probably pushing into places I shouldn't go, but I didn't feel right leaving just now. Despite the fact I didn't know Harper particularly well, she was important to Olivia who had essentially become the center of my best mate's universe. By extension of that, she mattered to me, even setting aside the draw I felt for her. I needed to make sure she was okay before I left her, and she'd been anything but since she'd laid eyes on that man in the park.

When the door opened, I held it and gestured Harper through, stepping just beyond the threshold myself. Stanley stood beside Harper, his eyes on her as if he was trying to ascertain her status. She stopped after several steps and hugged her arms around her waist, a visible shiver running through her. That's it. I was making tea.

"How about I make you some tea?" I asked.

Her eyes swung to mine, almost incredulous. "Tea?"

"Yes, tea. You're shivering, and I don't know what happened back there or who that man was, but it upset you. I'm British if you missed that detail, and us Brits happen to think tea makes everything better. At the least, it should warm you up a bit."

She stared at me for a beat and then smiled, just the smallest smile. "Okay. That would be nice," she said softly. For the first time since we'd seen that man, she seemed to relax a bit.

Her flat was on the small side. We'd entered into what must be the living room, which had a window taking up the entire side facing the street and offering a view of Puget Sound in the distance. Light fell in a shaft from the sun rising up above the water. The hardwood floor gleamed under the sun. A cream colored circular rug sat in the center of the room with a sectional couch surrounding it. A television was mounted on the wall above a small fireplace. The kitchen was to the side with an island demarcating the space from the living room. A door leading to a bathroom and another to what I presumed to be her bedroom were at the back.

She gestured to the kitchen. "By all means, make some tea."

It wasn't hard to figure out what was where, what with a tea kettle on her stove. With that and water, all we had to do was wait. It occurred to me I hadn't asked about the most important part. "I'm assuming you actually have some tea," I said, glancing to Harper who'd followed me around the island and was presently leaning against the counter. The lines of tension had eased on her face, and she finally looked back to herself. She grinned. "I do. Right over there," she said, pointing to a cabinet behind me.

I started to open it and then paused. "Is it okay if...?"

"Of course it's okay. If it wasn't okay, I'd have shooed you out already," she said with another grin.

I liked Harper grinning, liked it quite a lot.

———

HARPER

Alex Gordon, soccer star and sex symbol wrapped up in a body so yummy, he made me want to lick him all over, was standing in the kitchen in my new apartment making me tea. The incongruity of it made me almost laugh aloud, but I bit it back because he was being so sweet about the whole thing. He turned back to the cabinet and started rummaging through the tea boxes in there, eventually pulling out a box of, you guessed it, English breakfast tea. It was morning, and he was British. It made such perfect sense, I finally started laughing when he turned around with the box in hand.

Alex arched a brow, a smile playing at the corners of his mouth. "Something funny?" he asked, appearing slightly confused at my laughter.

If he was confused, well so was I, but I wasn't in the mood to ponder it. I had no sense of how much time had passed since I'd seen the man from many nightmares jogging our way in the park this morning, but thanks to Alex I'd managed to swat those feelings away. The relief was so great, it made me giddy. Well, that and the fact that Alex was here. Alex was so handsome, it bordered on ridiculous. He had brown hair that verged on curly and was often rumpled as it was now. Gorgeous honey brown eyes were paired with that hair. Beyond the fact he had a body that was all muscle and nothing else, the chiseled features of his face with classic cheekbones and a straight blade of a nose combined together to make him pure eye candy. To make matters worse, he appeared oblivious to his devastating effect on women and tended to be aloof and quiet.

I'd met Alex in passing through Olivia and her fiancée Liam. Olivia was one of my closest friends and had fallen hard for Liam Reed who happened to play for the Seattle Stars along with Alex and two other British soccer players. Alex was famous for his unshakable nerves under pressure as the goalkeeper, and thus far this season, he'd yet to let a goal from an opposing team into the net. I'd previously paid little attention to the international fervor over soccer, but Olivia had begun bringing me to games with her occasionally, so I had an idea of how compelling Alex was.

I hadn't let myself think much about how swoon-worthy he was, but right here, right now with him in my kitchen, it was hard to ignore. His presence up close was intense, yet comforting at once. He exuded a quiet power. Just now, I started to laugh again when I realized he was patiently waiting for me to answer. I pointed to the mugs I'd set on the counter, and he shook his head slightly as he stepped past me to drop tea bags in them. He turned and leaned his hips into the corner of the counter, just a foot or so away from me.

I sobered when it occurred to me I must seem half crazy to him. He happened to have been with me at an incredibly inopportune time there in the park. I didn't want him to think I needed protecting, although I was quite relieved he had been there and had guided me out of the park. With Stanley on one side and Alex on the other, I'd numbly made my way home. Alex's kind gesture of making tea snapped me out of where I'd gone inside. It was so funny to see this big, strong, powerful man offer to make tea.

I caught his eyes, like warm honey, and flutters swirled in my belly. I managed to take a breath. I felt strange—hyper-aware and restless. The awful truth behind why I'd gotten so scared this morning made me want to prove it had no effect on me anymore. We stared at each other, Alex's gaze coasting over me. He wasn't particularly easy to read, but I sensed an answering desire in him. My hands were curled on the edge of the counter, and I realized I was gripping it. I eased my grip and pushed away, my body humming and my mind driven to wipe out everything threatening to take over.

I stepped right in front of Alex, the heat of his body emanating. Getting close to him was like being beside a livewire—energy and power vibrated from him. His breath hissed when I stepped even closer. There was a part of me that thought I was completely out of my mind and perhaps I was. But dammit, I wasn't going to keep letting my life be ruled by one ugly incident. Alex was here and had magically turned my morning around. I wasn't letting this chance slide by.

With my pulse thundering in my ears and heat streaking through me, I slid a hand up Alex's arm. Oh wow. Just touching his arm was all kinds of amazing. He didn't move as I stroked over his muscles, savoring their feel of their strength and subtle power. His skin was warm to the touch and sleek. I didn't stop and coasted up over his t-shirt to curl around his neck. Thought fled, and I moved on instinct. His mouth was delectable with generous lips and a dimple just under his bottom lip. I curled my hand around his neck and pulled him toward me.

He stopped, maybe an inch away from me. "Harper?"

"Hm?"

"What are you doing?"

Excellent question, one that had layers of answers. The immediate one was all I considered. "Kissing you," I replied.

His honey brown gaze locked with mine, searching. I don't know what he saw there, but I could see the beat of his pulse in his neck, and his breath was shallow. Impatient, I yanked him to me. The moment our mouths collided, it was as if I'd been shocked. A hot jolt scored through me. He froze, and then looped his arms around me, pulling me up against him. Oh, this was perfect. Being held against his hard, hot body was heaven. He slid a palm up my back and curled it around my neck. Our kiss went from a stunning point of contact to a deep dive into pure deliciousness. I'd have guessed Alex to be a patient man, which made him an incredible kisser. He didn't rush and he didn't go all caveman and stuff his tongue down my throat. Oh no. He was slow and devastating with soft kisses, sweeps of his tongue against mine and nibbles on my bottom lip. All of it leading up to a kiss so melting, I truly would have collapsed had he not been holding me.

He drew back and tucked his head into the curve of my neck. I was relieved because I didn't know if I could bear to look at him just now. I'd meant to kiss him as some sort of bold move, as much for myself as anyone, to show I couldn't be cowed by the past. I hadn't known kissing Alex would be, well...a heady, encompassing madness that made me feel more alive than I'd ever felt. Eventually he lifted his head and eased his hold. I hadn't realized my feet had actually been off the ground until he slowly let me slide down his body. I could feel the ridge of his arousal against me, and my body's answering clench.

When my feet were on the ground again, I took a deep breath and stepped back. His eyes were waiting for me when I looked up. "What was that about?" he asked.

Excellent question. Right now, I wasn't so sure. "I wanted to kiss you," I finally said. A perfectly true answer, but it didn't capture everything I felt, certainly not the way I felt now.

He nodded just as the tea kettle whistled. The sound snapped the moment. Alex turned off the burner and poured tea. I slipped onto a stool by the counter and gestured for him to join me.

Available Now!

Big Win

Go here to sign up for information on new releases: http://jhcroixauthor.com/subscribe/

Brit Boys Sports Romance
The Play
Big Win
Out Of Bounds
Play Me
Naughty Wish
Swoon Series
This Crazy Love
Wait For Me
Break My Fall
Truly Madly Mine
Into The Fire Series
Burn For Me
Slow Burn
Burn So Bad
Hot Mess
Burn So Good
Sweet Fire
Play With Fire
Melt With You
Burn For You
Crash & Burn
Diamond Creek Alaska Novels
When Love Comes
Follow Love
Love Unbroken
Love Untamed
Tumble Into Love
Christmas Nights
Last Frontier Lodge Novels
Christmas on the Last Frontier
Love at Last
Just This Once
Falling Fast
Stay With Me
When We Fall

Hold Me Close
Crazy For You
Just Us
Catamount Lion Shifters
Protected Mate
Chosen Mate
Fated Mate
Destined Mate
A Catamount Christmas
The Lion Within
Lion Lost & Found

ACKNOWLEDGMENTS

To my hubby for fearless feedback on sports. To friends, near and far, who inspire me with every story because without friends life wouldn't be nearly as much fun. Many thanks to my editor for never being afraid to be ruthless with me. Yoly Cortez at Comar Covers blew me away with this cover - huge bow to her for her vision and creativity! To Croix's Crew, the most awesome group of readers a girl could ask for - thank you all from the bottom of my heart for your support!

xoxo

J.H. Croix

www.ingramcontent.com/pod-product-compliance
Lightning Source LLC
Chambersburg PA
CBHW070924190726
48292CB00004B/1094